Exquisite Mariposa

Exquisite Mariposa

a novel

FIONA ALISON DUNCAN

Soft Skull ✶ New York

Copyright © 2019 by Fiona Alison Duncan
First published in 2019 by Soft Skull

"I Want to Believe" © 2016 by Maggie Lee. Image courtesy of the Artist and Real Fine Arts, New York. Photograph by Joerg Lohse

Library of Congress Cataloging-in-Publication Data
Names: Duncan, Fiona Alison, author.
Title: Exquisite mariposa : a novel / Fiona Alison Duncan.
Description: New York : Soft Skull, 2019.
Identifiers: LCCN 2019008878 | ISBN 9781593765781 (pbk.)
Classification: LCC PS3604.U5268 E97 2019 | DDC 813/.6—dc23
LC record available at https://lccn.loc.gov/2019008878

Cover design & art direction by salu.io
Book design by Jordan Koluch

Published by Soft Skull Press
1140 Broadway, Suite 704
New York, NY 10001
www.softskull.com

Soft Skull titles are distributed to the trade by Publishers Group West
Phone: 866-400-5351

Printed in the United States of America
1 3 5 7 9 10 8 6 4 2

To Noo,

Who rescued who?

I have always been a girl.

I have never had a strong sense of reality because I'm a girl.

—KATHY ACKER, unpublished notebooks

Exquisite Mariposa

Episode 01—"Pilot"

THEY INVITED ME INTO THEIR home and within a week
I was discussing its telegenic potential with a reality show
producer responsible for nothing I'd heard of. The producer
was interested, and he wasn't the only one. "It's like *The Real
World* meets Instagram," cooed an ash-blond writer-curator. A
strawberry-blonde suggested selling it where I eventually did, to
this branding agency I'd worked with before. Their slogan: *Be
Human.* We were in one of Ed Ruscha's once-homes in Brent-
wood or Malibu, some far West forestial place, eating sanco-
cho, a Dominican stew our friend Rivington Starchild served
warm with whole avocados thanks to his mom, who coached
him through the family recipe over the phone. It was American
Thanksgiving. I was heartbroken, broke, and delighted with life,
telling everyone about the phenomenon I was sleeping in.

"There are three rooms, four beds, and five residents," I'd begin. "I'm subletting a bed in a room with two. I wake up next to this beauty—she's an oracle, I swear. All of these women, man. They're all so brilliant, so beautiful, and so different!"

The first night I hung out with Nadezhda she drove me between art openings on the back of her motorcycle. I'd silently promised my father I would never be a passenger on the back of any man's bike after he told me once about a woman he knew who'd died that way. But Nadezhda wasn't "any man." She was chiseled and statuesque with Soviet subway art tattooed on her right biceps. The night of our first ride, she was clandestinely young, twenty, a surprise I liked watching people register. People kept mistaking her for my big sister.

I didn't know to put the visor on my helmet down when we went over the highway. In the bathroom at Night Gallery, I found I'd amassed an eye mask of dirt. The art that night was predictably forgettable, unlike Nadezhda, who seemed to me like the matryoshka nesting dolls she kept on her desk, except every new layer revealed someone brighter and bolder. Later, she revealed she was terrified she would kill me. Her hands had cramped perilously as she gripped her '85 Honda handlebars. I learned, or remembered, because I should know this by now: *I have a tendency to see what I want to see.*

Nadezhda's apartment hallways were overripe banana yellow. Little white butterflies decorated the building's brick-red awning. The place was called La Mariposa, after the street where it was located. Two teenage girls were skating outside when I first walked up. Their black hair, which swished straight down to their sacra, flashed like mirrors in the sun.

I had been in Los Angeles for three weeks, trial living in my new friend Amalia's Koreatown studio while she was away at an art fair in London. Nadezhda lived nearby. Before I'd even arrived in LA, she had DM'd me an invitation to come over, which I ignored, because I didn't know her; she was a follower.

But then, I'd had the most exquisite three weeks. Night swims in heated pools, two beautiful new bedfellows, chauffeured rides through Laurel Canyon, long walks alone. Cigarettes were six bucks at the bodega, where plantain chips were sold in unmarked ziplocks and brain-sized avocados came ripe. Trees were flowering—it was October. I was feeling unusually trusting of what was coming to me, and more than that, I was dying to talk about it. So, on my second-to-last day in LA, I wrote back to Nadezhda, a girl with whom I shared no close mutuals.

None of her four roommates were home when I came by that first day, though their presence was evident in the knots of clothes on the floor. Nadezhda let me talktalktalk, which turned into dinner, a drive, and an offer-cum-plan. In two weeks, I'd return to live in La Mariposa temporarily as I looked for more permanent digs in my new crush, Los Angeles.

The first time I met Morgan she was eating dry flakes of nutritional yeast straight from the jar. She reminded me of my best friend, Simone, whom I had lived with in Montreal when we were around Morgan's age of 21.75. Simone and I had been roommates in an apartment we called "Hermie Island." We lived among moldering art installations, communal clothes, and several overflowing garbage and recycling bins. It was a long way out of the apartment—down a haunted staircase, past the neighbor who resented our borrowing a Persian rug of his we had found, through a snowbank in winter, mud in spring, and better-things-to-do in summer and fall, my happiest seasons in Montreal. Eventually, we dedicated a whole room to the trash we were too lazy to take out.

I guess I was nostalgic for this. I saw Hermie Island in Nadezhda, Morgan, and Co.'s household—in the mountains of bananas, the hall of mirrors, the dropout work ethic, and the frequent friend drop-ins. More than ten people owned keys to Hermie Island. At La Mariposa, I was introduced to new guests weekly. Like Jonas, an angel in thigh-high heels. And Mía, a beautician who'd make herself up like a train wreck, shading in bruises and liquid-lining cuts. Morgan was home less than some of these guests. She had a boyfriend with a place in Silver Lake, a car, and an ArtCenter degree to complete.

Alicia intimidated me. Composure does. Those who can pose. Alicia Novella Vasquez, aka @lightlicker, likes to shoot herself from below eye level. This angle imparts power. She told me she's wary of men who selfie from such a vantage point. (See: Adolf Hitler framed by Leni Riefenstahl.) All of the residents of La Mariposa are attentive to codes and slippages, the subtleties of self-presentation, especially online stuffs. They see beyond base programming, analyzing filters, comments, and composition, how often you post, in relation to whom, and with what probable intent, conscious or not. When I only knew *of* her, @com.passion was Alicia's Instagram handle. By the time I moved into a bed next to hers, she had become @lightlicker.

In person, I started to see how Alicia sees. Good models do that: they stare back. Alicia, which is pronounced with a *see*—not a *she*—at the center, has this intensity. Morgan says that's what all the residents of La Mariposa have in common: We sense. Intensely. That is, we're attuned to detail.

Take for example: Walking for pho one evening with Nadezhda and I, Alicia pointed to some writing on a wall on Wilshire Boulevard. In downtown Koreatown, below a Deco stone mural of three figures—a man in a tux, a man in a turban, and a woman dressed as a chef, her head bowed, one tit out—someone had scrawled: *You have 24 hours, Los Angeles & not 1 minute more, so(w) help me, God.* The paint was fresh-blood red. To the left of the three figures was more: *or do you need ANOTHER ACT of God to convince you?*

The three of us stood before the threatening words for a moment. Nadezhda's face was polka-dotted pale pink. She'd left the house with an acne-spot treatment on knowingly, like mock editorial beauty. The streetlights seemed to bend, aquamarine to teal. I remember thinking, *It's so like Alicia to spot something like this.* Alone, I probably would've walked right by.

I watched Alicia's gaze closely after that. Her irises scoured the world the way my little brother's did when I used to watch him read as a child—line by line, charging through new information. Months later, when I brought this moment up with Alicia, she told me, "The writing's still on the wall! Or at least the part that says"—I'd missed this—"'The only path to heaven is to transcend and ascend each and every time adversity strikes.'"

I wore Miffany's clothes while she was away. It was her bed I was subletting: $350 for three weeks. I think she made a profit off me. Balance it against the clothes I borrowed. A *Playboy*-logo hoodie, a shearling jacket, the bluest blue jeans. Her bed had four dense pillows and three fleece throws I'd wake up tangled in every morning. She hadn't made her bed before my arrival, which made me feel welcome, already in the fold. I'm trying to remember if I'd met Miffany IRL before I wore her clothes, but that's a thing about the now: Our selfies precede us. You may think you know me, but I don't even know me. Yes, we'd met. Once, in passing, at Gogo's show at the Ace. I was wearing a white Vejas dress the designer had gifted to me after Beyoncé's stylist returned it stained with makeup. I remember Miffany strutting in, a barbell in her belly button. September 2015, New York Fashion Week Spring/Summer 2016, just months before I took over her half room.

Miffany and Alicia shared what would have been the living room. Their beds were maybe six feet from each other, another six and you were in the kitchen, a few more to the front door. Safety-pinned sheets partitioned the space, poorly: permanent sleepover. I loved it. From Miffany's mattress, I'd look out over Koreatown to the Hollywood Hills. Every morning and night, through a series of cathedral-round windows, I'd pray to these sights: a high-rise crowned with the word EQUITABLE; another one, which read THE GAYLORD; and a billboard that said BADLANDS—the name of a publisher I was working with at the time.

Signs!

I was, and still am, very into reading signs. The world is full of them, and I'm full of it—convinced of reality's divine design, believing in magic, magnetism, the Wishing Machine, and maybe, that everything happens for a reason. That last bit I'm still skeptical of, as I am of "reason." I've experienced its exploitations and recognize its—or my perception's—limitations. I guess what I really believe is that it serves me to believe that everything happens for a reason, meaning-making being a reason, or a way, to live. I don't know! I'm shy to share existential meandering like this—intuitive, experience-sprung, flirting with flaky vocabularies—around most people. My father's a strict empiricist. At La Mariposa, though, I found a home for what I had long feared might be my lunacy.

(Did you know *lunacy* means "moonstruck," from the late Latin *lunaticus*? *Influence*, too, has an astrological root: "Emanation from the stars that acts upon one's character and destiny.")

In Alicia and Miffany's room, we'd talk about it all: infinity, etymology, astrology, spirituality, empathy, epigenetics, trauma, rape, race, class, sex, gender, technology, fashion, art, Justin Bieber, black holes, souls, *The Matrix*, fractals, spirit animals, family, branding, anxiety, the economy, conscious capitalism, collective consciousness, consciousness raising, Kundalini rising, twin flames, nail care, nicknames, rage, age, real estate, acid, Vine, love, and what we should make for dinner.

It was our talk I wished to capture. Truth seemed to be spoken nonstop from within this apartment. I loved how it flowed. One could join in and drop out at one's convenience or interest. Sometimes three of us would be talking at the same time and, somehow, we'd all still hear what the others had said. Often, another one of us, who we didn't think was listening, would chime in through a wall.

Our conversations, I felt, were in great contrast to the kind of talk trending online—the declarative, opining, often whining sharing on social media, which, for me, can individuate painfully, or twist into violent groupthink, bullying, and othering. Voice matters. Pitch and pace. More information is conveyed aurally/orally than in text. Hesitation, flirtation, pain, parroting, conviction, heart: One hears these things. I wanted the Internet—*everyone*—to hear us. That's what I told the girls: "I want to give you a platform."

I could visualize it, and so I thought it was right. That's what a famous R&B singer told me when I interviewed her at the Hotel Bel-Air: "I could see it all," she said, "like it had already happened, and so I knew my dreams would come true."

I saw us waking up before the camera. In the morning— or afternoon in Nadezhda's case—yes, but also like what I thought people meant when they used the word *woke*. That term was trending at the time. I've always been attuned to trend. After all, my parents cursed me with the initials *F.A.D.* I thought *woke* referred to a kind of consciousness, a mindfulness, an awareness of one's shadow and ego, a caution about our capacity for projection and delusion. I thought it meant an ability to perceive what was really going on, to situate oneself with regard to power, desire, economics, family, history, et cetera—to know oneself in relation to others, and *to act in kind.* It turns out many people were using the word to refer to someone who reads and can repeat trending news with a social justice bent. Even in their thinking, Americans are materialistic. La Mariposa wasn't, or not only. True, we loved fashion and music—broadcasting our taste. But all the women in this household also saw themselves as sharing states of becoming. And when we were home, we didn't fake anything. On the bus, we may have worn bitch faces to ward off male gazes. At part-time jobs, we probably smiled at shit we hated, because it was energy efficient. And online, we certainly pretended to be more successful than we were, because that was the game. But here, at La Mariposa, we allowed ourselves to process uncertainty. Fear! Nadezhda called it *an incubator.* "I like it," she said, "as a place girls come to, to grow to be themselves." Many of us have and will phase through; there are perennial subletters.

It was ready-made media. The apartment's themes were even reflected in its structure. There was a body—the living-cum-bedrooms/open kitchen—and to each side of that, two bedrooms—like wings! The layout of La Mariposa is like a butterfly.

All I saw were signs.

And then there's Max. I feel less bad about neglecting Max since he told me he deliberately dons a cloak of mystery. "I think I have more of a sense of who my housemates are than they do of me," he told me once over coffee. "I'm something of a withdrawn person."

Still, now, when I think of Max, I think of how little I know about him. Most of what I know has come through Nadezhda, whose room he shared. She called him her husband or wife, primary partner, roommate, boyfriend, friend. They met on a dating app in December 2014 when they were both nineteen. Max had been bumming around America: Alaska, New England, New York, Montana. He was passing through LA when he and Nadezhda matched. They went on a few dates, she says, "then he left, kind of into the void." Come summer he came back, and, "I told him he should move to LA, find some roots." He stayed in her room for five months, including the first three weeks I was there.

Maxime Flowers. Given name: Saoirse. His Instagram may be my favorite. It's all black and white, filled with cats, graphs, biblical snakes, requests for soup delivery, and poetry. Once I watched him edit a post. In under six seconds, with a single nimble finger, he edited a selfie unrecognizable except that it was in his signature degenerate grayscale. In person, Max speaks casually of *rockets propelling him* and *time as an abyss*. He has many twelfth-house placements. I've seen him wear a face of gold dust to a party. Topless under a fur coat, tight leather pants, foulards. His daytime look, when we lived together, was like *Hunky Dory* David Bowie.

During our only real one-to-one convo, Max informed me of a 1973 futurist text called *Up-Wingers*. It came up because we were talking transience, the nomadism La Mariposa supported.

"*Up-Wingers* is about a new living structure, the mobilia, based off jet-set, or hostel, travelers," Max explained. "It's a manifesto—" He paused. "I don't care much for manifestos." Still, he recommended this one. "If only because it's interesting," Max said, "to read what predictions for the future have come to pass. I find, for the most part, we overestimate our capacity for progress or velocity. We move a lot slower than anyone really hopes for."

Within a month of moving in, I had a contract drawn up for a "multimedia documentary exposé" on my brand-new beloveds and their communal home in Koreatown, Los Angeles. It would be *Reality Bites* meets Tumblr, *The Virgin Suicides* but healthful. *Young-Girl*, art world, recession America, *Survivor*! A real *Real World*. *The IRL World*. We would co-create it, social-mediate it. A trial in intersubjectivity. A critique of youth as commodity. A vision of zeitgeist *really embodied*. It would be truthful, lifelike, *amazing*.

"Why?" Nadezhda, the youngest beloved, asked shortly

after I signed the contract. I took another toke and felt my ego disassemble.

"I don't know," I replied.

Later, I would claim, "I just wanted to do what I always try to do, to share what I find beautiful."

Later still, I would bawl over my "sellout" "exhibitionist" "opportunistic" "incapable of real love" "fearful capitalist" animal instincts.

Why?

Why did I think to frame and display this place, these people, their privacy, for the whole world to see? Why was my first instinct to turn new relationships into paid labor? It was like the Hollywood hippie I called heartbreaker said: "Why can't you just be, Fi?"

It was in Morgan's underutilized bed that it dawned on me how truly fucked this reality show of mine might be. I woke up from an afternoon nap, midweek no doubt, still stoned, and saw her room for what it was: Real. The ceiling, the sunshine, the boxes of Pukka tea, the stacks of unwrapped chocolate, the crumpled hoodies, Simone de Beauvoir's *The Ethics of Ambiguity*—everything in there was Real.

This is difficult for me to explain.

I didn't use to believe in "the Real." Like in the Lacanian sense, or how Franco "Bifo" Berardi or Slavoj Žižek refer to it. Beyond the symbolic. I'd even published essays countering it. *Fantasy is Real*, I insisted. *Fake tits are as real at being fake as natural fat sacs are* . . . Which is true. But there's also: the Real. It's real. Indisputably now, *I know*. The Real is a mode of perception that makes all others seem like altered states. It's a mode I've been practicing living in. Microdosing psilocybin helps get me there, ditto a top-shelf indica, a hard-earned Savasana, the ocean, trees, and being with Amalia, Lucien, or Simone. The Real is like pure presence. Resistance-free. It feels like a shift to lucidity within the dream of waking life. It can look like a shift from 3- to 4-D. Space surpasses time as your prime dimension. Perhaps the defining characteristic of the Real is *not trying*. Like athletes and musicians say, it's when you're *in the flow*.

I know when I'm in and when I'm out of it—that's the most I can really say of the Real. Now I'm still more out than in. Mostly I'm in this in-between, knowing at least that I'm out, which is better than being wholly unconscious, which I've been—how embarrassing.

So I woke to the Real in Morgan's bed. It was a queasy awakening (first times tend to be). Truth rushed in like, *Hello, Nowness!* My real eyes realized "I" had been showboating. Seasick. Mental. I'd been projecting a *Hermie Island* sequel, this spin-off sitcom. *Californication, 90210, La Mariposa, Friends.* Situation comedies!? Bad girl, Fifi! It's the Situationist International you revere, remember? *Visibility is a trap. The revolution will not be televised.* Hollywood gobbled, I'd been scripted. *Damn, girl. LA. Hell A.* It hit me—

Why can't I just be?

Episode 02—*"It's a trap!"*

I BROKE THREE CONTRACTS IN 2016. The first was verbal, a monogamy clause. But he was fucking around too, and I knew, because everybody is psychic; I'd just become attuned to it. The second was an NDA. A man who gave me money asked me to sign it when we first met at the Hyatt near LAX. But he got my name wrong, took my Twitter handle for the real thing, so I signed smiling. The third and last was this reality show deal. Making a documentary about my new, younger friends and their home in Koreatown.

It's been one year since I signed my friends' lives away during my temporary stay, and two months since I officially joined their lease. As is the nature of La Mariposa, most of them have since flown the co-op. Morgan is living with her parents in the Bay. Alicia is in New York. Miffany's been all over. Ditto Max. I can't keep up. The only one left is Nadezhda, the one who initially brought me in.

Our relationship is sisterly. I never had one. She keeps asking me if I'm going to do something with this writing. I was sharing it with her and the other girls as it came to me, checking my mirror, so to speak. They consented yes, always. I was told I was trusted, which is a large part of why I knew I had to break our contract—I didn't want to risk compromising that.

In many ways, I feel even more than a year older now. I have been Saturn Returning, which is an astrological concept I'm no longer sure I believe in. I've spent much of the last two years trying to determine how *belief determines reality* and how much. Just last week a Kundalini instructor in Santa Monica speculated that one's beliefs manifest as event and circumstance. She was raised by a Vietnam-born mother, she said, who followed the Chinese zodiac. Her mother believed that those years forecast to be bad for her astrological sign would be. She feared them. And they turned out to be fearsome. "Looking back," the Kundalini instructor said, "you can see a pattern. The years my mother thought would be bad were—stress, calamity, loss. But I never believed. I don't know why, I always thought the idea was silly, that the Year of the Goat could be bad for me. I don't have bad years. My mother has retrospective proof of her belief. As do I. What's true? Maybe we make it up."

That's what my comic book artist ex-boyfriend thought of the afterlife: that what we believe it to be will be. Fire and brimstone? Heaven is a place on Earth? Gold-gated clouds? Absolute nothingness? Anything you want, you got it. I think he read it in a book.

Saturn is said to "return" when a person is between twenty-seven and a half and thirty years old. It happens again after another twenty-seven and a half to thirty years—for me, if I'm lucky enough to live that long. Western astrology is based on the belief that individuals, at birth, are imprinted with a set of influences emanating from the planets, stars, and other stellar bodies, which act upon one's character and destiny, determining stuff like how you communicate and experience beauty, your relationship to power, order, flora, fathers, and mothers. The planet Saturn is said to be Father Time, Kronos, dominating, reality-checking. He's cold, impersonal, and wise. And when he returns to the place in the sky where he was when you entered the world, he bullies you into your next life stage. Some don't make it out alive.

It's a fun game—asking elders what happened to them between ages twenty-seven and thirty. The stories tend to be epic: sudden career changes, international moves, surprise inheritances, marriages, divorces, deaths, births, travel, great works made and lost. So far I'm halfway through, and my changes have been mostly internal. Despite great effort on my part to shift my material circumstances, I am still chasing nominal freelance checks to pay rent, still loving boyish beings with suicidal tendencies, still plotting revenge on the capitalist patriarchy, and still fantasizing about never writing again.

Nothing has changed, and everything has. That's what happens when you come to believe in God. When you learn to be grateful to just be, every conscious moment in this realm, even loss and debt, feels like a gift. You sense, at least, that you're no longer afraid of death. Chronic time becomes illusive, a joke. The body is alien, an avatar, borrowed. The simplest actions bring pleasure. Walking. Cutting carrots. Sweeping cat litter. The sky is my favorite movie. This whole trip, though, is filmic. A play of shadow and light. Moment to moment to moment is Now. Forms change and there are essences that remain.

I call this living the Real. The more in it I am, the more like-minded lifers I attract. For a minute, I thought our reality show could be about that—about Millennials or Digital Natives or whatever you want to call us in our struggle to be Real. It's endemic in America.

Our apartment looks like a stage set. Something about its height and the light in LA. We're on the top floor overlooking parking garages and a cluster of high-rises. Beyond that are palm trees and the hills. Built on a slight incline, our apartment seems tilted forward from the entrance, threatening to descend into the concrete below. The place is painted pale institutional avocado and lime green, and decorated with the kind of cheap fixtures that look fake. Our ceilings are tall enough for a camera rig. Nadezhda now lives in what would be the living room were we not the kind of girls who tape posters to our walls declaring, WHAT DO WE WANT? NO JOBS! WHEN DO WE WANT THEM? NEVER!

As of today, we are three broke girls and a cat, Noo, a rescue who self-harms or self-soothes (maybe one and the same) by licking her ginger mane away. Her preferred haircut involves a shaved tail. Sometimes she'll follow that fade up her spine. The resulting look is like a reverse mohawk. Before I adopted her, Noo would hit skin and not stop. Now when I catch my cat manically licking, we play. I pet her and whisper, *You're so beautiful, you're so lovely, I love you, I will protect you, I promise you, you sweet divine, regal, beautiful creature.* A cat whisperer once told me to do this. "Cats are very vain," she said. (They are, epigenetically, royalty.)

I probably would've risked the reality show had the budget been better. But the youth culture industry relies on our selling ourselves short, on lit kids trading in their creativity, vitality, and taut-skinned desirability for a good party, tenuous social validation, and the false promise that cultural capital may translate in time to a source of real income. Many of us are happy to take the onetime check. A Calvin Klein campaign. Why not? Or maybe I'm a poor negotiator. My Saturn is afflicted in the second house of resources—money's the most mysterious thing to me.

Alexa K. was set to direct. The girls and I were stoked. Alexa is a real artist, market-vigilant or German-like, her cynicism services a sublime idealism. The branding agency said they couldn't afford her, though, even when Alexa said she'd do it for free.

At the time, I had been smoking so much weed my veins turned green. I had also been compulsively taking Voice Memos on my iPhone. Existential epiphanies, creative plots, intersubjective dialogues, and jokes—I felt the need to document it all. In one recording, I went off on what I was then calling *The Real Real World*, or *The IRL World*.

"Our show," I go, "it's about—"

How much of what I think I know was learned from media or other people versus from firsthand experience?

How many single images do I consume in a day?

Where do our beliefs come from and how do they organize our lives? Actions? Consequences?

If we were to watch what was going on in most offices, bedrooms, and homes, what would we see? What are we seeing?

Like, today I saw all over the world and back and forth in time. I was with friends in several countries. This is so cool, but what happens to the body when it thinks it's experiencing all of these adventures, romances, and horrors, but really it's sitting still?

It feels like we get flooded with the appropriate response stimuli to like, a physical threat or the wish to make love, but then ...

What are we doing with that energy?

If we could afford to adventure more offline, what would we do?

How would we feel?

Why are we poor? There's so much abundance about. Why are we pouring money into VR? Who cares.

WE ALREADY LIVE IN VIRTUAL REALITY.

We know so little of the machinations and magic of this realm. What is consciousness? The Real. Who said it ... that quote ...

[Thumbs through iPhone.]

Few women ever experience themselves as real. —*Andrea Dworkin*

Oh brother.

But really—why don't I feel real? What makes me feel real? Mass shooters don't feel real. We want to have influence. We seek to test reality. Ripple. Ripple.

Actions have consequences.

I feel Real when I talk about the Real with other people. Sometimes.

You can't look more than one person in the eyes at the same time.

Why is there so much suffering? When it could be so simple. IT IS

SO SIMPLE.

I have all these beautiful, brilliant friends and family. WE'RE HERE.

Right now. Alive.

Yet we're stressed and depressed and some say lonely or lost.

Why do all these kids write to me saying they're lost?

The show is for them. What if we collected them? In one place where we could learn to recognize each other. Learn to Be. Truthfully. Mirror mirror. The world is a mirror. Don't you see?

I had been walking around Koreatown alone taking these oral notes. It was late. My period had just come on and she was wavy. A mournful orchestra of milky, knotted energy was rising from my pelvis, its notes culminating meters beyond my body. I sat on an apartment stoop on South Harvard Boulevard to finish my monologue. Becoming conscious of where I was and what I was doing, I started to describe the scene around me: the full moon, the oceanic traffic sounds, a nearby Dr. Seussian garden, and all the passersby who looked oblivious to my madness. (Few of us out here allow ourselves to really recognize one another.) As my tearful in-breaths became laughter, I felt the same channel-change as in Morgan's bedroom. It was as if my eyes widened, letting in more light. Depth chiseled the edges of my vision. The movie clunked into 4-D. I'd gotten there. To this blessed realm that my friend Clara, who we'll come back to later, had been breaching too. Once, at a farmers market, Clara and I got there together. I remember Clara turning to me and saying, "Some people live here!" The Real. "It's really real!"

When I first moved into La Mariposa, among its six residents, including myself, our three-room apartment housed twelve different kinds of eating disorders, stacks of unopened letters from debt collectors, racks' worth of Goodwill treasures, and drawers full of stolen Sephora. We had addictions: to fuckboy drama, selfies and likes, deli wine, cardio, and anything oral. We shared desires: for True Love and Universal Basic Income. Our traumas: the psychic schism of routine objectification (body dysmorphia, surveillance paranoia); over-media-ation (mercury poisoning and ADHD); date rape (dissociation, anorgasmia); debt and joblessness (insecurity, anxiety, and shame); and parental migrations, depressions, deaths, addictions, and divorce (attachment and abandonment issues). This was all out there. Talked about. Art was made about it. It decorated our floors and walls. After living in New York for four years, where the "artists" I met were so professional—rich kids, groomed to continue to profit—I was refreshed by the candor, idealism, diversity, and genuine artistic talent I witnessed in this Los Angeles home.

I met the residents of La Mariposa at that age where differences of class and related values start to show themselves. When you're young, in your teens and early twenties, in an arts scene, you can all seem the same. Everyone spends everything they have. Living in a dump is just like, you party a lot and don't care to clean. You can process crap food, drugs, and alcohol, and still have radiant skin. You look cute in everything. As you age, this begins to change. Around twenty-seven, I started to notice who could afford to have babies, buy houses, and invest in their careers, who had the start-up capital and contacts to launch a small business, buy canvas, hire assistants, and travel. And who couldn't—who got sick and disappeared. I realized all these kids I'd hung around with at parties in New York City came from low-key dynasties. Politicians' kids, CEOs' kids, famous artists' kids.

I wanted to belong. Before I knew what was going on, I thought it was possible. I remember being out to dinner—I was twenty-four and had just moved to New York—with some new friends in a neighborhood called NoLIta, where rent on studio apartments was $2.5K easy, and every other shop was staffed by Australian fitness models. I was always tense at these things, choosing the cheapest wine and saying I wasn't hungry, when really I just couldn't afford the steak my anemic body craved; I ate from the bread baskets others ignored. I didn't understand how everyone could go out all the time, and live where they did, and look as they did. Radiant! At this dinner, I remember, a typical NoLIta clique walked by, models and girls who trained to look like models, and I said, "Everyone is so beautiful here!" And my friend Susan, who was always right, replied, "No. They're just rich."

"Oh." I swallowed the moment, not fully processing it until

just recently, when it dawned on me that these people weren't, as I'd thought, better than me at what we did. I thought they'd earned their wealth by working harder and being smarter and more innately creative, talented, graceful, and godly than me. Worthier. When really, America's class system is a caste system. At this point in capitalist history, wealth has consolidated such that class mobility is anomalous and still: the promise.

It's like we're all forced to play this rigged game of Monopoly where some of us start off with a little stack of money and one property, some with stacks of money the height of hotels, a few run the bank, and many are in jail. Money, in this game, is no longer just paper, it's coded numbers on screens that most of us aren't educated to read, let alone trade in. And the rules of this game—they keep changing. People who consider themselves "winners," those who can afford to, make up the rules as they go. They make deals with each other and the bank, to suit their established interests, to win all the wealth.

(The earliest version of Monopoly was known as the Land-lord's Game, patented in 1904.)

Money, now, can buy so much. It can buy beauty. You wouldn't believe the subtle cosmetic procedures the daughters of socialites I know get. Money can buy a false sense of desirability. A majority of my friends have escorted, dated, or otherwise traded their genetic beauty for cash, which is dangerous—the delusion of a man paying for it, his repression, resentment, and rage. Money can buy you a career in the arts. Once I started paying attention, it became obvious—how many young so-called creatives, from painters to magazine editors, were just uninspired rich kids. I wonder if they thought I was one of them, the trust-funders and hangers-on I spent time with.

I met the first lot through my model friend Cupie. The rich are impressionable to beauty. I'm not beautiful enough to qualify on looks alone, but I have taste. Impeccable, covetable—even salable—taste in theater, art, music, literature, and most of all: fashion. I love clothes! I'll be the homeless woman talking to the sun by the Pacific Coast Highway in a vintage Lagerfeld blazer, Fiorucci jeans, Yves Saint Laurent hat, and Lucchese cowboy boots—they're embroidered with flaming phoenixes, eternally returning in style.

"Oh, you're just Canadian—" is how well-to-do Americans write me off when I get all rah-rah class-conscious lately.

"I can't believe it's like this!" I exclaim. "And y'all accept it?"

But I didn't know it. Not when I moved to New York and worked ninety hours a week at various gigs trying to keep up with the cool kids. Not when I experienced a masochistic mental breakdown from the inevitable burnout. Not when I rehabilitated care of yoga and other healing-industry goods. And not even when I killed our reality show contract, mostly because I was ashamed I couldn't negotiate a livable budget. I still thought it was my fault. I still believed "success" was based on merit. On True Talent. And that I didn't have it.

Of course, at the same time, I also didn't believe all that. That's the thing—it's like deep-dish-pizza down *we always know*. Even when we can't articulate it, or act on it, we know what's true, just, and beautiful. What's Real. Love. Our souls will it, which is why we have so much mental illness, cruelty, and violence in our culture. Our true natures are repressed by manufactured desires and fears, by the temptation/frustration cycle of consumerism and power-as-domination. It's like my sixty-nine-year-old mentor Steven Klein says, "The ego industry is a mass conglomerate!" You will never be satisfied.

Even when I was a teenage camp counselor, I couldn't help it: I always played favorites. At La Mariposa, I loved Alicia's art the most. One of my many jobs in New York was to report on hype things for "cool" magazines. I was always looking for a feeling, a spark, someone putting experiences into forms until then unexpressed. If the magazines I worked for back in New York were really cool, they would've put Alicia on the cover, and assigned me to profile her for a good three thousand words, but these outlets aren't after what they pretend to be. Like authenticity and art—they act like that's their deal, when really they're looking for accreditation and validation. Trading in existing cultural capital, they don't know how to generate it. Real artists are generators, not traders. My editors were always asking where else my proposed subjects had been reported on; how many social media followers they had; and/or what famous people they'd collaborated with or were born from. There's a checklist. Alicia doesn't qualify—yet.

When I was subletting the bed next to hers, Alicia was always churning out images—digital collages, fashion editorials, portraits, still lifes, and videos—that reflected the violence of desire, attachment, and healing. That feeling of wanting to destroy the one you love. To consume them. Knowing you're acting evil and watching yourself do it anyway because you don't believe in the goodness of yourself, or because you're attached to people who behave the same way. Alicia was especially good on loving men—masculine hetero men. She figured animal sex. Instinct, aggression, and loyalty. Divinity. Looks of abduction, eyes blackened. Her manicured nails looked like blades and shields. There was melancholy and beatitude.

Even in my dArkest, Alicia once captioned one of her Instagram posts, *there sparks burning in my mouth,* which is as concise a description of her work as I can come up with.

I wanted to see what Alicia would do with a budget. It's hard to say who was the most broke among our lot. It would've been a difference of a couple hundred bucks a month, which to us was a lot. In Los Angeles, Alicia patched together rent from miscellaneous bartending and modeling gigs, which got her out of the apartment. Otherwise she was at home, which was affordable. Alicia made art the way I did when I first started: from need, love, and naivete. When the feelings are as big as the information is chaotic, you put it into physical form in order to better see it, rearrange it, and maybe change it. Computers and their offshoot tools, like editing apps and social media, had given Alicia a near-free medium to work with. Grateful for this, Alicia constantly gave all her work away for free on social media. Her giveaways were more interesting than most movies being made, but they were ephemeral, diffuse, not reaching all they could touch. While they were helping her process, packaged like this, they weren't going to build her the artistic career she said she wanted.

I wanted to help. Blame my Virgoan servitude, my bleeding Leo Moon heart, and my burgeoning maternal instinct—and maybe also, I was projecting. You know the myth of discovery? Someone sees in you something you can't see yourself or don't have the resources to cultivate, and they make it happen for you. Classic story, the crafting of a leading lady. When I was younger, I so wanted that to happen to me. Soon after I signed the contract, enacting the part of discoverer, I realized how sick that story is. Casting agents, headhunters, and commercial producers are opportunistic creeps. What I envisioned for Alicia and the rest of La Mariposa, for our show, was less creepy than it was delusional. I was attempting to put on their oxygen masks before I did my own. I was faking it, so they could make it. Nadezhda did this, and it drove me crazy: she performed the role of "hacker girl," when she only knew basic html. (Even I bought it for a minute; the girl dressed and talked the part.) I had fancied myself as a patron of the arts, like my second-wealthiest friend, Henry Gaylord-Cohen, was always telling me: "You'd make the best rich person, Fiona." Clad in vintage Mugler and local handcrafted clothes by Lou Dallas, I would throw Jean Stein—worthy dinner parties; fund-raise for sexual liberty, affordable housing, right-to-water, and education; and you know I'd collect the heaven, hell, and Earth out of Real artists.

Now in New York, waitressing full-time and so tired, Alicia's pretty much stopped making work. Many of the best are striving in the shadows. Spotlight's full of frauds.

Episode 03—"Love loves to love love"

THE OTHER NIGHT LUCIEN CALLED to talk about our relationship. When he tells me he loves me, I say I can't feel it. "If only you believed . . ." he repeats, leaving me to fill in the blank. I can feel my love for him. When I meditate, this patient rush will come spreading through my heart center, and I have angel wings. This is Real. And when we're together, in person, and I can lock eyes with him, or hold him, then I can feel it.

But he's only intermittently here. He's like my favorite TV shows from when I was a teenager, before streaming on-demand: I only get him once a week, on his schedule. Predictably romantic and always ending with a cliff-hanger, I'm left longing for more. Usually I wait patiently between episodes, because I've come to think—and because he tells me this is so—that his absences are deliberate lessons in restraint, self-knowledge, and

God. And I do experience heavenly ecstasy in the waiting, when I "stay in my heart," as he tells me to. But then sometimes, when there's a longer gap in our programming, my mind will start to believe all these other things. He doesn't really see me—know me—love me. How could he? What's there to love? I pick fights and act out; drama, lies, cheating. He insists he's faithful, equating godliness with monogamy, and suggests I work on my faith.

We've been on and off for a year and a half.

The night of his call, I was in what used to be Nadezhda's bedroom, where I now live with Noo. It had been weeks since our last conversation. When I told him I'd been struggling— lacking work, money, him—he asked if he could read me something. Lucien prefaced his reading by saying it had been his mother, who he knows I admire, who first shared the piece with him.

"It's a letter by Rilke," he said. "Written from Rome. This one is fairly common. Maybe you've read it?"

I hadn't. Lucien always seems to share exactly what I need. The perfect song, a myth, a memory. It's one of the things I love most about him. He tells me it keeps him coming back to me, despite the repeated hurt. "I communicate more beautifully with you than with any other," he says. "But you—" Often, I have to tell him, *I'm not really here right now.*

The letter was about love and solitude and men and women. Individuals must "become world," Rilke writes. We must learn to live in our solitude—to ripen and cohere—before we can really be with another. *I know, I've been trying,* I thought. Because I know if I don't, I'll continue to use men and media to fill my void. Feeling my influence—how I can delight—that makes me feel Real for a minute. Performing sexy or cute, dream girl, bad girl, generous, bratty, mother, savior, sweet. It's so retrograde, but I love fulfilling these roles, witnessing how even Lucien, who claims to want me to be this autonomous Rilkean woman, buckles under the pressure of his boner when I pout, or how he warms when I listen rapt to his monologues, the problematics of which (his classist judgments, for instance) I only clock in retrospect, when I'm alone again.

In the letter, Rilke writes about "the girl and the woman in their new, individual unfolding." Dumbstruck and identifying, I started bawling as Lucien read the following:

Women, in whom life lingers and dwells more immediately, more fruitfully, and more confidently, must surely have become riper and more human in their depths than light, easygoing man, who is not pulled down beneath the surface of life by the weight of any bodily fruit and who, arrogant and hasty, undervalues what he thinks he loves ... someday there will be girls and women whose name will no longer mean the mere opposite of the male, but something in itself, something that makes one think not of any complement and limit, but only life and reality: the female human being.

Playing the role of guru, Lucien read this letter as a riddle, offering no interpretation of his own. We hung up with *I love you*'s, and I lay down in my bed, a hand-me-down mattress on the floor, which I'd been sharing with dog-eared library books and maps and charts—plots to fix the world. I'd been drawing these maps, of histories of technology, of wealth as it's distributed now, of value systems and where I fit in, all to try to figure out how I might help enact some kind of change that would bring me a life I could like. A life that would allow me to be Real 24/7.

That Lucien read *that letter* seemed as prophetic as the letter itself. According to my charts, Western women have been stuck in this phase that Rilke described as "imitating male behaviors, misbehaviors, and male professions" for half a century, if not more. I want independence as much as the next girl, but I don't want to have to fake bossiness, bitchiness, ruthlessness, or self-ishness, or sell my sexiness, to get it; that's a trap. So I stay in bed. But Rilke got me all revved up.

"Tomorrow, I will leave the apartment!" I declared. "But to-night, just a poem—"

And so, at the top of a convoluted map on "the advent and dissolution of private property," I wrote this guy:

She who opposes
> *force with counter-*
>> *force alone*
>> *forms that which she*
> *opposes and is*
>> *formed by it.*

In the desert last year, shortly after I killed our reality contract, I took mushrooms with this kind boy I'd been dating for three weeks named David. I felt in love with both him and Lucien at the time. I'd been sleeping with the two of them, sometimes both in the same day. Neither of them knew. David seemed to offer what Lucien lacked and Lucien, fucking Lucien—I kind of hated him then. I felt like I could say anything to David and he'd get it or at least try. While everything Lucien said felt like *It*: godsent, genius. I envied him. Articulate and persuasive, with friends in high places (Lucien's mother was famous), the kid lived my fantasy: sleeping under a Cy Twombly, he only diaried on hotel stationery, as he traveled frequently to Moscow, Buenos Aires, Paris. The desert was basically his backyard—he, only twenty-six, had been glamping in it for decades.

I'd been microdosing mushrooms for months, so I was familiar with the trip. The feeling of lungs like wood. Breathing slow as a tree. My feet on the ground, every step a massage. The concrete or sand or soil beneath just as much a part of me as my heart, whose simple knowing would finally hush my brutal, greedy mind.

In the desert, I stretched on a rock as David played jazz saxophone while his friend Sofia coiled herself in copper sheets. They were in art school, and this performance was purportedly why dozens of young people had congregated in the desert, but from my stoned perch, it looked like Sofia was doing it for the photographs; David because he was generous, or unsure of himself, and Sofia had asked; while the rest of us were there for the beer and party favors.

After the performance, I ate more mushrooms. In David's car, en route to the campsite, I sat on his cute friend Milo's lap and psychically had sex with both him and David, who was driving. I thought I was planting seeds for later in the tent, but when we got to the campsite, David and I walked into the desert. I'd

never seen so many stars and I was obsessed with the spaces in
between. They seemed to represent suffering or a natural emptiness we fear to plumb and so suffer from. Birth, death, the
womb, void. It was cold and impersonal and universal, and I understood how I was host to it.

David was having a great time. In the dark blue his face became a mask of birds and then a lizard. He laid a blanket down and
we had sex on it. I had visions of myself as a painting by Marjorie
Cameron. Split tongue out, on my knees, cat-cowing. *I'm Inanna*,
I thought. There were slithers. *I am the Earth.* "But don't forget"—I
remembered Lucien saying—"at her center, Earth is Fire."

After—what? Did we cum? I can't remember. I was the
Universe until David started talking—why did he have to start
talking about what a shame it was that few people still practiced
the art of oral storytelling? That's Lucien's art. It's one of the
things I love most about him. I thought: *I should be here with
Lucien.* The Sky chimed in, "When you try to have everything,
you end up with nothing!"

I told David I was "gnarly tripping." He didn't let it bum his
high down. I loved that about him. David is trustworthy, kind,
and self-caring. I started shaking then about the stars and the
alphabet—how language organizes, how reality may be a col-
laborative script, how if only we'd author it more responsibly,
blah blah blah—and David said he could tell I was onto something, that most everything he'd heard from me seemed to be
geared toward this something, and it felt real and worthy and
like it was going somewhere. I cried. David held me in his arms
and told me I was really, really special.

"And," he said, "I don't think you know it."

I'm nothing, I thought, not self-pitying, not pleading for attention, like I had so many times before. It was just true, free-feeling.

Why do few women ever experience themselves as Real? All my life, or at least since puberty, it's been easy for me to see that others were alive and hard for me to feel it except in extremes— feeling fatally beautiful, getting hurt, loving like it's a service. This led to crisis.

Most of the women in my life seem to be similarly afflicted. We have anxiety disorders, depressions, bipolar swings, and furies. We wear cosmetic defenses, like BB cream and over-compensatory intellect. High achievers, my girls are public successes, even famed. But I've seen them in their living rooms, with hollow cheeks and sallow skin, telling me that if they didn't perform as they do, they'd kill themselves, and that they're convinced they're dying or will soon, anyway, which is probably true, if they think it.

When I met the women of La Mariposa, maybe because they were younger and better at faking bravery—or maybe because I'd spent the six months prior in a retreat of self-care where I had visions, real experiences of true freedom and creativity—I thought we could make something great together. As I got to know them, though, I realized these young women were a lot like *I still am*: limitingly self-conscious or prone to self-protective falsity in public, which now, thanks to social media, all feels like *publicity*. We effusively interrogated our passions in private, but feared that none of it would be taken seriously by the powers that be.

We weren't ready to make something Real together. Nadezhda was controlling. Almost dictatorial in her distaste, she could list all these things our reality show shouldn't be but offered no alternative vision. Meanwhile, Morgan froze. At our first and only photo shoot, I melted all the more in love with her. The branding agency had sent a photographer to the apartment. Before the camera, Morgan, who is Andreja Pejić–striking with big attentive eyes, jujube-plump lips, and a long straight nose, didn't know how to hold her face. She looked as though she had mean gas, which she might've—we both get IBS when tense. I couldn't stop laughing at her sweet impossibility. When we got the pictures back, no one looked like themselves. Nadezhda loaded a group shot in Photoshop and swapped everybody's heads around so Max grinned above Miffany's cleavage and Morgan farted on Alicia's music-video-babe frame. Sharing it in our group chat, every room in the apartment laughed.

I want to take my beautiful, brilliant friends' pain away. I want to eat it like I do my feelings, slathered in nut butter, and then shit it in the form of writing. (Everything I write is shit—why do I think this?) I want my friends to breathe easy, to recognize their genius and not take it personally, to feel loved, not like they have the world to prove, and to nurture fearlessly—there's this sense we'll be exploited if we care too much, especially about men, so we other, blame, and rarely let our guards down. Most of all, I just want us to be able to hang out and make stuff without going into the trauma. We talk so much about what hurts.

Language-free experiences are rare for me. I like to converse—it's a big part of my social life and work—but I love love *love* feeling free of words even more! That's my ultimate Real. When I'm spinning on news cycles (headlines stick like pop refrains), my mind often summons this visual: I'll fold rooms full of pastel cashmere sweaters.

I practice taming the voices daily by repeating mantras, stretching my heart above my head, painting, singing, meditating, and the bad habits: smoking, binge eating. I was a low-key sex addict for a while because sex was the first exercise I found that would shut the voices up. The voices, the voices. Sometimes they're beautiful, but it can be too much! In New York, where I lived for almost four years, I heard e V e R y T h i N g. Police choppers, screaming, gossip, honking, put-downs, ads, and catcalls. *Ass so fat you can see it from the front, Hey red, wanna ride on, So I texted then he texted then I texted then, Can I take your picture for a Japanese style blog? My agent says, It's just like when you've got some coffee that's too black, which means it's too strong. What you do? You integrate it with cream—you make it weak, Next stop Canal Street, That'll be $26.18. $454.14. $2.99. $106.66. $12.80. $9,000. I can feel your halo (halo) halo, I can see your halo (halo) halo, our tears!*

The loudest voices are real-world silent. Like inner bullying and my paranoia—sometimes I think I know what everyone's thinking: the subtext of conversations, the motivations behind actions; these come through without my wanting them. People tell me shit—maybe that's it. I hear it again and again: "I don't know why I'm telling you this," or: "I've never told anyone this before." Maybe I'm unconsciously asking for it. I don't really say anything, but I listen.

This is all to say that sometimes I become so full of voices, I've considered smashing my head on my apartment's brick walls to make them stop. Or I'll climb as high as I can go and scream because it's not just voices, it's The Words.

Sitting on La Mariposa's roof one afternoon, wanting to just be, my senses bounced all over on the scene naming: *Azure, Queen palm, Jacaranda, Airplane Airplane Airplane, Streeeeeam, Mockingbird mocking car alarms, Roses, Thorns, Pricks, When roses are delivered, they shave off the pricks, Dicks, I Love, Gratuitous, Lascivious, Luscious, Limits, Cerulean, Fire ants, Sting, All wisdom is remembering. Shut Up!!*

Kissing Lucien, this all gets quiet, so I love him. I'm drawn into a trance from the way our tongues dance. When we hug, his breath gets long and loud, reminding me I have lungs too, and when he moans, it's with repose, like how he tells stories, like he's never worried about wasting someone else's time. I'm practically mute in his presence; I don't want to interrupt; the intel is too valuable; I'm routinely dumbstruck. God, how I love going out of my mind!

Freud believed something like, *Traumatized people don't remember their trauma, they reenact it.* I'm not sure what happened to me to make me so crazy. My crazy being: not being Real. I fake a lot. Lucien calls me phony when I don't sound like myself. On the phone, he'll say, "Can I talk to Fiona, please?" (Miles Davis said [or so the Internet says he said], "Man, sometimes it takes you a long time to sound like yourself.")

I've had dreams of child molestation. Sometimes it's my younger brother who I've failed to protect. Once it was me. I have no waking memory of this happening, but I have few memories of life before ten. I don't know if it matters what happened. Past is past is fiction like future. While the now just is—if I meditate on that, I can get free. Suddenly, the channel will change. And I can just be. Often, though, I catch myself acting out scripts and plotting fantasies to fulfill. I write my reality. Desires manifest. This is cool when it's conscious, but we have underworlds within. When you find yourself in the same situations and relationship dynamics again and again, that's a sign!

A few months ago, I ate an award-winning cannabis candy called Cheeba Chews. This was the only time in recent memory when, having none, I would yearn for words. Can a hallucination be guttural, sensational? This experience wasn't visual, not beyond splotches of colors and a penis-like form. I was lying on Nadezhda's shearling throw in the middle of a vacant Mariposa, unable to open my eyes. What I experienced had no setting or plot. Characters, yes—or a person, someone I know, but I'll never tell who. The feeling: inescapable burning shame and a shamefully pubic turn-on. Suffocation. Familiarity. A disgusting, sticky, sick shame *raged*.

The look was that of light coming through squeezed-shut eyelids, I later realized. Red, pink, and black light flickering obscurely. I couldn't escape the feeling.

Engulfed, I thought maybe it was a memory of Nadezhda's. She experienced rape in young adulthood. Or maybe a collective consciousness of sexual trauma. It could be birth—the first sexual trauma. I let myself explore it. I wanted to be brave, to see if I could touch the truth. Does it matter if it really happened? Wasn't this stoned summoning real enough? The feeling was of a child sexually used by an elder. I couldn't move. Was it me? Was it a repressed—or could it be, a false—memory?

I imagined my Jungian analyst's cat-lined eyes lighting up, extra-compassionate, hearing about how I may have been sexually abused, as if she'd discovered a cracked black obsidian egg up my—

But isn't that what she's trained to look for? Childhood sexual abuse is *the story* of trauma and healing. Have we been set up? Did Freud really reveal something common, or did he script it into our cultural consciousness? It also occurred to me, paralyzed on Nadezhda's throw, that this could be a media memory. I've watched enough episodes of *CSI* and *Law & Order: SVU*, re-watched *Mysterious Skin*, and read Heather Lewis—maybe I'd confused those stories as my own, embellishing. My imagination is such that, last year at Joshua Tree, a Burner type was tightrope walking ten stories above me, and though I was sitting on the ground, I swear I could feel the wind on his skin.

I called my friend Susan. She said, "It's not real, you're stoned."

Susan has this certainty about reality: Drug experiences are not real. Only sober, live, immediate, here, now, a priori experience seems to be "real" for her. She's a performance artist. Up until then, I'd considered everything as real. Every hallucination, projection, dream, fantasy, and magazine story—all were part of my vision of reality. It's multidimensional. REALms.

A month after my bad Cheeba trip, Nadezhda invited over a boy she wanted to sleep with. Jordan's the type who's stoked for virtual reality; he said he'd happily trade in his body for programmatic freedom. Nadezhda was twenty-one to his thirty-something. It was late afternoon on a Sunday. I was in my bedroom as usual, when Nadezhda, feeling shy in her seduction, asked if I'd join their hang.

We sat in the exact same place on Nadezhda's floor where I'd gone under. Jordan offered to smoke us up. As he rolled a spliff, I explained my decline, omitting any real details: "I don't want a bad trip again."

"Bad trips bring up stuff we need to work through," Jordan suggested.

"Of course," I replied. "But I'm not ready . . ."

Jordan smoked alone on our roof. When he came back down, Nadezhda showed us an iceberg graph of conspiracy theories she had found on the Internet that she thought we might like. On the triangle above the water it said: *9/11 was an inside job, The Illuminati,* and *The US elections were rigged.* Underwater was: *The Holocaust was faked, Michelle Obama has a dick,* and *The Earth is flat.* Even lower: *The Roman Empire still persists, Satan controls the Earth,* and as deep as you could go was: *Reality is Story.*

"That's what I believe!" I exclaimed.

Episode 04—"It's a trap!!"

THE BRANDING AGENCY'S OFFICE WAS in the East Village. Three floors of high rent. The company was founded by a bro, some early-thirties white son of money who wore streetwear and a Rolex. The company made its money creating "brand experiences" for other companies: fashion labels, boutique hotels, cosmetic conglomerates, and the occasional car thing. "Brand experiences" meaning parties, fashion films, social media ad campaigns, pop-up shops, and artist collaborations—the kind of insidious advertising that tries to pass as generous, artful, and authentic. For "creatives" by "creatives." The work looked like popular art from the eighties, street style from the nineties, and Internet trends two years too late. Up to ten interns worked there at a time. One of their unpaid tasks was to troll social media for "inspiration." They'd screengrab what cool kids were wearing and sharing, then present it as market research.

When I first moved in to La Mariposa, my new friends were already being ripped off by this agency. I thought: might as well cash in.

The agency had a "culture" front. They'd finance little not-ad projects to look like they cared, like an interactive whaling tour of Hawaii, a map of Bushwick delis, and our reality TV show. I'd worked with this agency before. I wrote their Books column when I lived in New York. Imagine fifty bucks for a four-hundred-word column (typical rate), and $1K in rent. At one point, it felt like buckets of words were being funneled down my throat. Letters have sharp edges! Choking hazard! And my intestinal tract—*devastated*.

The first budget the agency offered us for the show was okay. Meager split between the six of us, but since we were all pretty much otherwise unemployed, the few thousand was exciting: *something to work with*. It kept getting cut, though. Then it was no Alexa, they wanted us to work with one of their commercial directors. Fuck no. We settled instead on doing it ourselves. Shooting on all our cell phones, we'd bring the footage together at the end, like a great Exquisite Corpse. A trial in intersubjectivity! Merging our Realities! *MirrorrorriM MirrorrorriM on the screens, what does it mean to be seen?* I loved the idea of a Real Life social experiment we'd then edit into TV.

The unknown made the branding agency, and some of the Mariposa girls, nervous, though. Nadezhda was accustomed to preplanning all her selfies. Her commanding self-consciousness

extended to public dialogues, in which she'd assert grand state-
ments, masking the personal with conceptual knowledge, or
she'd act mute, observing with obvious judgment. She spent
half her childhood in Russia—she has trust issues. Morgan,
meanwhile, was unaccustomed to being seen at all beyond the
Real Real. She didn't like to put her form on display or use the
tools common to our age. No selfies. They freaked her out. "But
maybe that's a good thing," she said. "Maybe that's why I should
do this?" The branding agency, of course, wanted the product
in advance. That's how advertising works: you pitch an existing
idea, then execute it precisely.

"Tell me," Alexandre, my main contact at the branding
agency, said at the outset of our first and last office meeting,
"who are these girls?" (Everyone always forgot about Max.)
"Who are these characters?"

"They're not characters!" I said. "They're real people—
infinite, ever-changing, composed of generations of genetics and
the histories we've been taught, of every experience we've had, of
our dreams—where do they come from? Why do they feel . . .
so solid?"

"Right," Alexandre said. "But that doesn't help us. We don't
know them. You have to introduce us to them. Here, let's play
a game—"

He wrote down the names of all the residents of La Mariposa, one of them incorrectly, on a piece of scrap paper. He
pointed to the first one.

"Anastasia," he said. "Who is she? In one word, describe
Anastasia."

"Nadezhda. And no."

"Just try."

I closed my eyes and summoned Nadezhda. Her face is china-doll symmetrical, creaseless and refined, as if photoshopped. When she smiles, which is usually with a laugh, you get to see gums and crowded teeth, mischievous wrinkles burst on every side of her pale blue eyes. Her smile is gawky like how she dances, not like you'd expect, thin limbs noodling from elbows and knees, her solid core pogoing as her head cranks from side to side. Nadezhda can be mean, deliberately so it sometimes seems. She'll ask you about your greatest insecurity as you're walking out the door to a job interview, or she'll bring up the similarities between your ex and your new lover in front of the new one. She's a shit disturber, just like my dad used to call me. A punk. Nadezhda and I could be sisters. She threatens my prideful ego like one—repeatedly cutting me down to humility. But then she can be so compassionate and wise, offering better counsel than my Jungian psychotherapist ever has. Nadezhda diaries daily in eight-point font, likes trompe l'oeil clothing, hoards stationery supplies, throws temper tantrums, and learns fast. Growing up in Russia, the foundation of her English came from reading and writing rather than speech so she'll sometimes pronounce words funny, like *ka-veet* for *caveat*. She was twenty when I first met her, and she's fated, I'm certain, to make way more money and material-world difference than I ever will. Stubborn, willful, judgmental, and justly intentioned ...

"A force," I said.

"How so?"

"Forceful, um . . . Dictatorial. Like the Brain in *Pinky and the Brain.*"

"Great!" Alexandre wrote *the Brain* next to the name *Anastasia.*

He had me do this for every "character." Alicia was reduced to *the Sphinx*, Miffany to *the Muse*, and Morgan to *the Hard Body*. Alexandre's list had the same aura as that group shot from our first photo shoot. A dysphoric almost-likeness: *MirrOr mIrrOr.*

I felt like puking, and then Alexandre made a proposition: "What if," he said, "we placed this brand-new very cool Australian ginger beer in a bunch of scenes in the show? We just signed with them. They're . . ."

I'd tuned out at "Australian." It was so funny—I'd already seen this movie! It's called *Reality Bites*, from 1994, directed by Ben Stiller. It's one big ad for the Big Gulp. ("Why can't you just be, Fi!?")

"You're the devil!" I exclaimed. "This is pure evil!"

Alexandre smiled. I liked him a lot. He had an education in neuroscience, a French wife, and a fat newborn. I thought for a minute. *Evil is in devil, just as God is in good.*

"I would accept," I pronounced in my bullshittiest voice, "a sponsorship from Bragg Premium Nutritional Yeast, or *Vogue.*"

An hour later, Miffany walked into the Chinatown dumpling parlor I'd reserved for our interview. I'd been conducting one-on-one interviews with all the members of La Mariposa. This early research was designed to guide my role as the creator and host of our show. Miffany—who'd been in New York for two weeks, overeating in a dark apartment with a friend who, she said, was "really going through it"—was the last on my list. It was snowing outside and Miffany was wearing an XXL T-shirt over an XL hoodie with rave-wide corduroys and thin shimmery jewelry.

"Aren't you—"

"Cold, yeah."

In Ottawa, Ontario—fall/winter 2001—I wore a uniform of JNCO raver jeans, cropped tank tops, and a faux-fur parka from Abercrombie & Fitch that didn't cover my midriff. Every day, I'd arrive to computer class, first period, grade eight, with the bottom ten inches of my jeans frozen solid. They'd melt inside, soaking my Airwalks and socks. I was dressing for post-surf SoCal in minus-twenty-degree Canada. (That's minus four Fahrenheit.) My parents called me a fashion victim, and I pouted back: "You just don't understand!" They didn't. They couldn't remember that kids don't feel the cold. My belly would be pink from exposure, and I didn't feel it. I felt cool.

I served Miffany hot tea and ordered Chinese broccoli. Since it was her bed I was subletting, I knew her the least well. Also, maybe because she was seemingly the most girly. Until recently, I've had a hard time connecting with girly girls, maybe because I'm often told I'm girly myself. I don't feel it. *Girly* is vapid, frivolous, and dangerous, ripe for exploitation—or so I was raised to compute. I knew how girly girls were judged and dismissed, as if we hadn't given this yawning world a good think, as if we were *asking for it.*

What I am that might come across as *girly*—being gentle, dressing in ruffles with exposed lace lingerie, luxuriating in pastel, giggles, grooming, and gossip—is actually rooted in great wisdom. It comes from a recognition that the power games that pass for intellect, strength, and import in this world are rote, wasteful, and ouroboran in their chase. Lonely, oppressive. *Seriousness.* No thanks. Life is short! And beautiful. Water's like liquid crystal. I wear a rose quartz egg up my pussy every few days to connect with my heart chakra. Tongue kissing vortexes me through the cosmos. Dry brushing your skin before showering enlivens the senses. Moisturizing too. And as the great spiritualist Jean Vanier knew: *The closer we are to the body, the closer we are to spirit ... relationship is hand-to-hand, eye-to-eye ... the Word became flesh, God became flesh.*

I knew all this and still a part of me circa thirteen to twenty-eight judged others who acted *girly* in public—talking only about relationships, for instance, with little lilts at the ends of their sentences—if they hadn't also figured out a means to money and/or other measures of consensus reality power because *that is dangerous.* I know how *Just a Girl* codes are read, and lately, I'm performing them all the more exaggeratedly because of it, even when it's to my detriment. Lucien diagnosed it: Oppositional Defiant Disorder.

I wish I'd known better than to judge the likes of Miffany. I wish I'd known since forever how little judgments reveal about the objects of their scrutiny—it's on us, baby.

Miffany and I sat at a corner table between two windows in the dumpling parlor. Condensation had collected on the glass. As soon as she sat down, Miffany started doodling into it. Little naked devils with round butts and no genitals, butterflies, and what looked like doughnuts and a deconstructed American flag surrounded our tiny table, which was now crowded with slurpy rice noodles, shrimp dumplings, steamed pork, and fried sesame buns. Miffany didn't order or touch any food until I noticed and said, "I'm charging it to the agency." A lie worth every penny.

I didn't know what to interview Miffany about until she started talking about what I'm usually too ashamed to: boyfriends. (Classic girl talk.) My Lucien and her Josh, their substance abuse and subtle abuse, and how we loved them regardless. We talked about how it could be "spiritually productive" to be in a "low-key abusive" relationship, a way to work through familial and cultural trauma. "The sex is so good!" (When it also hurts.) At the time, we both thought we were "actualizing through their gendered ignorance."

"It's like Josh and I are the same soul," Miffany said, locking eyes with me with such intensity that I was just like: "*Totally.*"

"But he keeps trying to make me his mother!"

"Ugh. I know. Like Lucien says he wants to, but he doesn't get *how* to love my soon-to-be woman. Before Lucien, I always had like, educated, older lovers. Now I'm having to learn to explain my priorities, desires, and boundaries. It's actually help-ing me in business negotiations."

"Ha ha!"

The most astounding revelation of my conversation with Miffany—and this was always happening at La Mariposa: my diseases, habits, and pain articulated as gendered and cultural as I learned I wasn't alone—came during a talk about body dys-morphia. Miffany was "feeling disgusting" from all the "trash snacking" she'd been doing these last few weeks.

"I know I haven't put on weight," she said. "But I *feel* out of shape, and I have to remind myself, that's okay. Don't obsess"— because when she used to, and this has happened to me too—"I would *feel* like I *was* a Hans Bellmer doll." Every limb was a thigh, her breasts and belly ballooning and multiplying, until she was just orbs and orbs. She'd float out of the room, or she'd shrink into a spit bubble that would pop in her own mouth, and then she couldn't eat at all.

Body dysmorphia, as we experienced it, is beyond low self-esteem. It's not about not loving our bodies, the answer to that being: *Every body is beautiful, equal opportunity objectification.* No, this disease came from a recognition of the truth that *We are not the body,* without the embrace of it being practiced. When you're granted so much attention for your form, and you like aspects of that—validation, *I exist!*—it's easy to get confused: to mistake the form for the feeling, the body for the being. You can get su-perficial. Self-objectify. Let men and media, who assume *you are your body,* use it, and so: *What does that make you?*

Lucky for us, the body is wise, a messenger. It will act up, in an attempt to wake us up, if our minds give in to falsity, like if you accept and repeat the language virus: *You are your body, little girly.*

Miffany told me that about a year ago, when she was living at La Mariposa, partying a lot, and working part-time at a juice shop, she had started seeing from a God's-eye perspective. Outside of herself. Vertiginous.

She'd been tooling around with makeup, trying to diet on free juice, and daydreaming of real careers. "I was bored, I didn't know what to do," she said. "I thought if I looked better, my life would be better."

She became obsessed and, once the idea crept in, it took over. The language virus had Miffany caking on makeup and skipping even juice meals as her body clammed up in acne and started holding water in weird ways.

You can't control me, the body retaliated, *can't wield the world this way!*

The language virus wanted her to be seen as the ideal of beauty, but she—her Realest of Real she—didn't want to be seen like that. She wanted eye to eye, God as flesh.

"It got so bad," Miffany said. "I would try to go where I used to be fine, like to the same parties, with the same friends, but *I wouldn't be there.* Later, when I would try and remember the party, I realized I couldn't picture myself there, I couldn't fathom my body in a room. I didn't know what conversations I had, who I was talking to, my mouth moved but ..."

It was as if her spirit had fled the scene, and Miffany couldn't see through all the shade and noise, the assumed judgments, *who's looking at who*. The language virus had Miffany trying to see herself through everyone else's perspective, those being imaginary though—not Real. More like magazine gazes and beauty contests. Close-ups of celebrity cellulite on rags in the grocery store checkout line. *Hot or Not. Who Wore It Better*. Hierarchies of beauty fortifying class divides. If she'd been calm enough to receive it, Miffany and I agreed, she would've felt beautiful, as in loved, how those around her loved her.

This is why I feared being a girl and being close with other girly girls. You have to be vigilant in engaging with *girly* or else its associated language viruses can infect you. There are so many ideas of what a girl means—false ideas repeated to consensus. Even if you were raised to question them, they get inside of you, they organize your thinking and doing, your being. For a long time, I tried to inoculate myself against these viruses by repudiating the feminine. I wore my hair short. Didn't flirt. I was hyperrational. *Cool*. And then someone fucked me like a woman and all that blocked Mother Nature, fatal-femme energy rose, and since then, I've been day-by-day learning to revere my femininity, while surviving in this dickhole reality. I'm terrified of being taken advantage of.

Before I left for New York, Alicia had told me the one thing she didn't want was for our show to be marketed "as anything even related to a sleepover." During our meeting at the branding agency, I relayed this to Alexandre, who replied, "Sure."

When I got back to LA, I received an e-mail from Alexandre with his notes from our meeting. Cc'd were four male names I recognized from the agency's contact page. The subject line was: "Cool Girls Sleepover :)". I marked the e-mail unread and crawled into bed.

Episode 05—"F is for Fake"

HOW DOES THE REAL FEEL? Every time I get there, it feels like a landing, like *Earth to Fiona*. It's humiliating, because you know it was there all along. We're in it even when we're not. Like, you've seen someone drunk, right? Their sloshy speech, clumsy limbs, and lizardly libido, and you're sober, at least with regards to alcohol. The Real's like being so sober, you realize that anything can be an intoxicant. Stories are, and characters. Ego trips. Social pressure. Most people are out here tripping on their own personal cocktail. What's your fix?

Throughout my teens, I dosed on straight girlfriends and straight As. In my twenties, I tried everything I could think of: nicotine, sugar, amphetamines, psilocybin, LSD, ecstasy, cannabis, Valium, Xanax, DMT, alcohol, sobriety, monogamy, polyamory, abstinence, sluttiness, sleeping until noon, rising with the sun, semesters off, one B- (in a seminar called "Boys Dudes Men," duh), raving, lazing, waitressing, publishing, traveling, volunteering, sugar babying, consumerism, Buddhism, masochism, vengeful feminism, feminist solidarity, Catholic studying, popular science studying, workaholic-ing, like Mom, like Dad, Protestant work ethic unlearning, queering, neo-Marxism, New Ageism, Taoism, fashion journalism. I tried Ludwig Wittgenstein, Brian Greene, Richard Dawkins, Camille Paglia, Susan Sontag, James Baldwin, Alan Watts, Sun Ra, Philip K. Dick, Courtney Love, Chris Kraus, Durga Chew-Bose, the Quran, and on and on. I tried way too hard.

Before I moved to Los Angeles, after spending a summer in Toronto, I was almost twenty-eight, growing my hair long for the first time since fifteen and having vivid dreams. My dreams often feel as real or more real than waking life. I got off for the first time in a dream—this, when I was an anxiously anorgasmic sexuality studies major. A month later, I orgasmed with a partner. Repeatedly, my dreams have awakened me to true possibility.

It is a fact that no one wants to hear about other people's dreams. It's like we can't even. When I'm reading Jung, whose work I otherwise love, as soon as he starts detailing a dream, the letters get all scrambled, it's just weird shapes on a page. Given this psychic block, let's pretend this dream was Real Life, because that's how it felt.

It was the night before my flight to LA, and I was a wife and mother, like my mother's mother, a stay-at-home mom. It was the 1950s. My dress was hard to run in, and I was fleeing. Dear life. I sprinted out of my suburban bungalow into the front yard, barefoot and screaming, as my husband pursued me with hands to kill. Not an uncommon scene—cinematic—but what was unusual was the feeling. Sometimes in dreams, as in Real Life, you register little sensation. Other times, like in this nightmare, you're re-sensitized: the most decadent feels seem to flow beyond your control. I screamed, knowing no neighbors would help as panic fired my limbs to fight. Scattered, searching for my children, my heart hurting so precisely—it was Real enough to wake me up, changed. I understood something now that I hadn't before. And I knew it had something to do with my new long hair.

The thing I hate about being a woman is how I'm made to be one. On Themyscira, Wonder Woman's Paradise Island, hair is just hair, a natural outgrowth of the Divine, like everything else. On Earth, it's a signal to harass us. When I had short or shaved hair, if I got hit on, it was as an equal or a revered one; almost everyone I dated identified as queer. I started growing my hair out during my last year in New York when my budget became about spending close to nothing. Now I attract Republicans.

The last man I fucked was this Australian model who party plans for Peter Thiel. I met him at a sex party in the Hills, and since everything is relative, he seemed great. Both there "by accident," we made fun of the scene until we were a part of it, fucking in a darkened corner of a garden mezzanine, overlooking all of LA. It was good for me—he had a beautiful cock and practiced stamina (she-comes-first manners)—but then, when we met again, he was all like, "My friends tell me I should marry you." I know I'm kind of asking for it by the way I behave—simple, sweet, *and* perverted. (Fake.) ("You're cool *and* hot," a different bimbo once said, astounded, "fun *and* smart." "Yeah, I know," I replied, "I work really hard on being ideal so I don't kill myself." I.e., I'm insecure.)

After the marriage scare, I ignored the Thiel guy's texts for a week, but answered his call.

"It's shit or get off the pot, Fiona!" he said, trying to bully me into hanging out.

"I've always hated that expression," I replied.

Does this work for you guys? I'd never been treated like a thing a man can corral before LA and the hair.

In the months before I moved to Los Angeles, I was also experiencing hallucinations while meditating. I wonder if hallucinations, like dreams, aren't made to share—will you receive them? These hallucinations were full picture shows. My eyes were closed as I watched scenes stream as if on an IMAX that was tapped into my nervous system. I didn't have to do anything but observe. I had been consciously practicing being more receptive. The Tao was teaching me how. *Honor your yin, your dark matter, the feminine.* I wanted to walk the Way.

The way I'd been moving through life before—willful and reactive, in drag, or mute, shy—had inspired duress. In the years prior, I'd been panic attacked and suicidal; addiction-prone, yearning, manic, and then bitchy, lonely, and ashamed. I was vain, and so, as had happened with Miffany, my spirit sought to rouse me to

Reality by challenging the body: I got acne, rashes, allergies, fevers, gas, and unusually dispersed weight gain. I was sick.

Now I was getting better thanks to a new language virus: *I give up!* I couldn't care anymore about things I used to, like developing a career, pleasing men, looking good, or even having a home. I was crashing where I could, relying on the kindness of others. Working as little as my hunger could afford, I studied astrology, Eastern religions, and magical esoterica as self-help, and learned to meditate via yoga. A common scene (*Eat Pray Embarrassing!*), but I didn't care, because of the feeling.

I'd started to smell like I hadn't since twelve, maybe thirteen. Humid and elemental, it was the smell of spontaneity. *Pierce that thick cloud of unknowing with a sharp dart of longing love!* I just was. Still often anxious but learning to ground down. I hadn't yet met the Real—that humiliating bliss—but these months were like foreplay for that climax. Sometimes, it takes us a long time to get there.

The two most persuasive hallucinations occurred within a week of each other. During the first, I was in a queer yoga studio, guided into restorative poses, with props all around me, as an elderly woman walked around performing Reiki. During Savasana, our final corpse pose, I'd experienced a feeling of total safety unremembered since kindergarten: I was a child about to nap on a mat.

Calm and alert, body at ease, my mind summoned, in visual detail, all these scenes of Fiona aching, from puberty to the present. I watched my past play for me, in a series of medium and long shots, all these moments where I had betrayed some inner knowing. This knowing was represented by a second me, who acted upon my past reality. I kissed the top of my head. Put the blade down. Walked away from the car. Apologized. Made tea. Tucked myself in. Made love with myself—sweet, gorgeous love, the kind that's both fast and slow, reassuring whispers and carnal gropes, every move instinctual. Fiona on Fiona :P

The uncanny thing was "I" wasn't doing any of this. The more my active mind surrendered, the more memories were summoned and taken care of. I watched in titillating awe, and understood how, in every masochistic moment, I'd always known what better to do.

The second hallucination took place on a sunny afternoon. August 14, 2015. I was told, by a man livestreaming on my computer, to close the curtains, turn off the lights, and lie down with a soft cover over my eyes. For forty-five minutes, he guided me and a thousand-odd others around the world in a meditation into the Underworld. We were figured as Inanna, a Sumerian goddess of love, sex, procreativity, and war. As Inanna, we ventured through a forest to a tree with a door. Through the door, we descended down flights of stairs, stripped of all vestments, until we hit hell. There we were killed and laid on a cool stone table. Each of our organs was inspected, cleansed, and put back. People I'd loved, like exes and great aunts, visited me as my liver was washed and my heart massaged. (I paid eleven dollars for this livestream, timed to a Leo New Moon.)

The surprise was Ash, a girl I'd half-consciously competed with in high school, whose bare, engorged breasts I'd once caught a side view of. At the time, the desire had been so strong, I imprisoned it. Ash was the leader of our five-girl clique. We didn't do drugs, watched our drinks, got straight As, and were virgins. We played board games and planned field trips to do activities like skiing and sailing. I was the group outlier. I read feminist erotica and comic books, liked punk music, and had a history as a bad girl. Tween Fi offered boys double-tongue blow jobs, holding her best friend's hand. At thirteen, I went good—joining this clique—after my great-aunt died. Bad-girl Fifi didn't go away though. She'd sneak out occasionally, flirting lasciviously with younger-grade members of the football team, or making comments to the clique about clits. This seemed to disturb my friends. They'd "ew," and once one of the girls told me, "You better not be a lesbian."

So I had loved Ash. Inanna made this obvious. I had loved her romantically, sensually, devotedly. Any ill feelings I had held—like resenting Ash's frigidity and perfectionism, her Katie Holmes looks back when Katie was more famous than Michelle Williams, and her innate understanding of math and science, like my father, who was so impressed by her—were but a shadow of the love. I really did love Ashley Anne Cooper. And this was okay. It was beautiful, actually.

Recognizing this, beauty surrounded me. It energetically lifted me, like for Real. My chest rose from the floor, neck and jaw too, until my upper body crested, making a half-moon of empty space between it and the floor. Orgasmic feelings waved in, out, and around my core, piercing my limbs and holding me up. I felt an ecstatic calm culminating in a great bliss like I'd never heard anyone speak of or write about. For three or five or who-knows-how-many minutes, I was lifted, while bright white light poured through my still-covered eyelids.

I've come to believe this was what's called an "energy orgasm," the first of many I've had since. It was maybe also my "Kundalini awakening." (A snake lies dormant, coiled at the base of our spine—our Chi, Eros, vital *mmmm yummm me* God-given energy—waiting to rise. The meditation was, I later learned, led by a Kundalini instructor.)

Since this experience, what I most want is to get pregnant. If I had to act a sad part, all I'd need to do to cry onstage is think about this new life that may never come from me. Longing tears for suckling babes cleanse my face regularly. The desire is so deliriously motivating, I've basically stopped smoking, and the reality show deal, I see now, in retrospect, probably came in part from it. My instinct to nurture these people younger than me, *and* to get me some money. That's the only reason I'll publish this story, if I ever do—I'll sell my soul to get the money it takes to raise a family.

I had told Lucien I was moving to LA for him. I had told myself it was to research a book on my latest obsessions: Kundalini yoga, Western astrology, and other New Ageisms. I grew up in a household, the ideals of which I followed into my canonical Great Books undergrad, where such *flaky, unsubstantiated quackery* was derided. What I discovered in singing Sanskrit mantras, breathing into my heart, and charting astral maps was great practical knowledge—cures for my diseases. I'd started to suspect that the derision of New Ageism was misogynistic and imperialist, marginalizing truths we should rather honor. I still wanted to be validated by the people and institutions who raised me, though, so, instead of just enjoying practicing yoga and astrology, I rationalized it into work.

As I prepared to leave Toronto, this was my plan: I would study the New Age movement, its history and contemporary practice, its scientific research, and its language viruses, from its hotbed of Los Angeles. I would go *undercover*, immersing myself in this world, with the excuse of a popular text I would then write and publish to save myself from the dead-end career I thought I was in.

What I ended up doing instead was an even greater Los Angeles cliché: I fell madly in love with the child of one of my favorite celebrities and started working in TV!

Lucien's mother was a great dancer, poet, and painter, someone who straddled popularity and esoterica. Her name was spoken often at our family dinner table in Canada because my parents loved to tell my origin story: "You were conceived in an early Frank Gehry house in Point Dume, Malibu. Our next-door neighbor was . . ." Lucien's mother.

"The night I met your mother at a Venice Beach bar," my dad would recount, "she got drunk and dropped her only dollar bill in the toilet. She fished it out and paid her tab with it." This charmed him, as did the fact that: "She was the first woman I met who could eat a whole box of Chips Ahoy! in one sitting."

My parents moved to Canada when my mom was eight months pregnant. They were twenty-seven and thirty, artists who couldn't afford to give birth in the US. Lately, Dad likes to tell me they immigrated because of politics.

"We left Los Angeles the year people started shooting up freeways for no apparent reason, and it's only gotten worse."

My parents wish I'd "come home," but Los Angeles is my home. I understood, within a week of being here, why people fight over land, how you can feel so attached to a parcel of earth, you'd risk dumb shit for it.

Lucien's mother bought the house I was conceived in the year after my parents left. Two years later, Lucien was born. He lived there, in this house that was storied to me, until he was twenty. This is just one of many coincidences we'd later read as *serendipity*. He'll say it's like he doodled me and there I was: his dream girl. I'll say the same, but it was writing. I wrote him: my destiny. Lucien tore Reality open for me more than any other. He decimated my ego, and I loved it.

Our relationship was more than low-key abusive at times. *I went from believing I would have your children*, Lucien once texted me, *to now absolutely fucking hating you. I should honestly slap you hard across the face.*

Part of me loved Lucien's verbal abuse, the same Oppositional Defiant part who would cheat on him, convinced he was doing the same. (He was.) It's not exactly the same part of me that's writing this, well-knowing that Lucien may see it as the ultimate betrayal, which I get. I was cautious with our love, respecting his privacy, slow to commit. I wanted to be sure that I loved him-him, not what he was born into. (People use famous people like they do hot women—objectifying, flattering, worshipping, manipulating, and getting off as they cut us down.) I do. Love him. I've consulted every organ of my being, in every state of being, and no matter the mood: I love him. We have this elemental connection: eye to eye, flesh as God. I pray daily that the world delivers all the beauty, knowledge, and happiness possible to that little fucker. One of the smartest and most sensitive creatures I've met, and tortured. So cute!

Part of me also recognizes, though, that my love may be Stockholm syndrome. Lucien's not the only patriarchally diseased boy I've been turned on by. (The morning of Trump's election, I found myself ramming a red jasper dildo up me to channel our new president's Chi.) I get off *fiercely* abusing abusive boys. I take my hatred of patriarchy out on them one by one—making them fall in love with me and then crushing them with swift breakups excused because "I'm a feminist and you're not." Instead of schooling the boys in all the insidious things they've done, I let my resentment quietly build until I can no longer take it, then I'll shout, "Read a book!" and I'm gone.

Lucien discerned this in me early on and called it out. "Kali dominator." "Feminist punisher." "I'm not your punching bag, Fiona," he said. "I only take it because I love you—"

"I LOVE YOU!" he used to scream, as if saying it was enough. "Let me love you! Let me love you!"

(Every concurrent Justin Bieber hit was a theme to our early relationship. "Sorry." "What Do You Mean?" "Love Yourself." "I'll Show You." It was charming at first—the songs were always on the radio—but it's time to grow up.)

Lucien has repeatedly told me the reason he wants to be with me, and only me, is because he's already done "the fuck everything thing." Once he told me he used to call it "bag over the head" sex. He could sleep with anyone if he pictured a bag over her head. "But it felt horrible, Fi," he moaned. "I never want to do that again."

Lucien's beheading confession was so fucked-up and banal. Typical LA fuckboy. Hollywood dreamboat predator. Equally fucked-up, though, was how my body, instead of reacting in disgust, was turned on. I took to fantasizing about sitting on Lucien's face, smothering his golden-boy beauty under my goddess squat, or picturing him with other women: his whimper, our power. I cum so easy and BIG for this kid. For the last year of our on-again off-again, I've pretty much masturbated to Lucien exclusively. Even when I was with other people, I thought of him. And mostly, my fantasy was of the reality of our lovemaking. Our connection, beneath all the rubble of gendered conflict, is soulful. We Tantra together. It's wild! Sacred Energy eXchange. Our lovemaking is so sweet. "I love you I love you I love you," we repeat. It's Lucien's babies I want. If only he'd wise up.

But what about me? When will I wise out of my patterning? Attracted to friction, I don't go for lovers who are plainly good to me. I like to be pushed around too much, beaten even. The first "great sex" I had left me covered in delicious bruises. An easy explanation is that I was beaten as a child. I remember once being spanked in front of my friends at my sixth birthday party. I'd been loud, bratty, acting out—I can't remember why. I do remember I was deliberately escalating the conflict with my father though. I knew what was coming, because this was our pattern, but it wasn't the public spanking that upset me, nor was it the sting from my biggest toenail getting caught on a doorframe and torn off as my tiny body was swung around the room and into his lap—it was that he let *that* happen. It was his *inattention*.

Episode 06—"Simone"

ONE OF THE PREMISES OF Western astrology is that we choose our lives, the time and place of our birth, and our parentage. Harmony, a dancer I know, says this is true in African cosmology too. Life is like a game we set ourselves up to play. We select certain givens—the imprint of celestial bodies, in astrology—which direct our play, to a point. When I was in my pre-LA healing phase, I found this idea empowering. Some greater *I* than "I" could totally discern *chose this for me.* Canada; parents who never said "I love you"; a tendency to self-sabotage; and a body built for gymnastics: I chose these, pre-destinies. This meant that, beyond my Earthbound personality, the constructed nature of which bored me (*Just a Girl, brought to you by Imperialist White Supremacist Capitalist Patriarchy*), there was ... a soul? A me-being who was free!

It meant I wasn't victim to the bullshit of consensus reality. I was, rather, an active player in a game of life I'd decided to play in my own particular way. Maybe I'd even chosen to be brainwashed! *Stockholm Syndrome, brought to you by the soul of Fiona Alison Duncan.*

This explained why a part of me was entertained by my pain. Why reality felt so ephemeral; *The Matrix* glitches, déjà vu, and premonitions. It even explained my yogic hallucinations. There was a part of me—a loving-light part, unstuck from ego—who knew what better to do in all situations. My own guardian angel. Supreme Fi.

I saw the study of astrology as a way to self-actualize into this higher-level self. If I understood the patterns of my personality— like how my Leo Moon, my emotional center, is magnetic, playful, and showy, and can make me fall in love with almost anyone, and vice versa; but is also victim to illusion, vanity, and pride—then, maybe, I could evolve into the best Fi I could be.

I tend to join trends as they're cresting—I told you I was cursed with the initials *F.A.D.* Astrology's gone in and out of style before; right now, it's peaking in popularity, because people are desperate for a meaning system more nourishing than capitalism. I joined this wave of interest two years before my move to LA. In 2013, after being introduced to the art and science by a couple of committed esoterics, my astrological birth chart became my cheat sheet and rule book, a secret guide I consulted constantly. I started studying those of friends and family, cities and celebrities.

Every sign in the zodiac, I learned, has levels of actualization.

We can act like victims to our own inclinations, or we can make the most of them. We can be annoyed by others' oddities, we can manipulate and take advantage of them, or we can nurture, honor, and love them. For example, Virgo is famously exacting—a potentially brittle perfectionist (Beyoncé) and a bitch to be around (Mother Teresa)—because she has access to the divine. This level of perfection is not possible on Earth, though, except through her imagination. She can't enact it here, which, if she's unaware of this, will frustrate her, as she works tirelessly to an impossible standard. But Virgo can, in her visionary determination, get us as close to divine beauty and justice as Earth's gravity will allow. Virgo must learn to love the perfection of imperfection, our here and now. We must encourage her to take it easy. Organizationally shrewd, she clocks linear time so effortlessly, one of Virgo's duties is to learn to relax and forget about it, like Pisces, her sister sign, who swims in eternal currents. I learned that everyone has every sign, house, and celestial body in their chart, and that each chart is unique. We're all made up of the same stuff, in different proportion and weight.

Another premise of Western astrology is that we're living out past-life karma and early childhood trauma until thirty. Our progressed Lunar Return at twenty-seven and our Saturn Return from around twenty-seven and a half to thirty are rites of passage—energetic and material obstacle courses designed to free us of the past and/or make it obvious, so we can integrate nature-nurture-soul-whatever, and move on and into: a Real adult life. Survival habits, ego facades, and buried hurt are *supposed* to come to the fore during this period. We start to see how we've been patterned, what has and hasn't worked, or what doesn't anymore. We become more refined, or picky: knowing more clearly what we want and don't want, and how we might get it or not get it. You can't account for everything, though, and that's one thing I've learned: how marvelous it is to surrender to the unknown.

My best friend from Canada was Returning twenty months ahead of me. Simone, which is pronounced like *see-Moan-ay*, and I haven't lived in the same city since we lived at Hermie Island, but as she'd say, "The island is a state of mind." We text every day.

As a rascal teen, Simone was a semi-pro rock climber. She lived in a van after high school with a much older boyfriend, also a climber. They drove around North America, scaling rock faces and selling weed. Then Simone went to art school. She studied painting, sculpture, and art history. Her father, who she hadn't seen in years (he lived off the grid on an island near Honduras), died near the end of her studies. After graduating, Simone, like me, hung around Montreal doing almost nothing. That's when we got close. We'd bike around that adult playground of a city, so accustomed to laughing we started doing it for its own sake. "What's funny??" "I don't know!" We'd laugh until, every once in a while, one of us would pee our shorts. When this phase—as phases do—waned, Simone moved back to her hippie hometown of Guelph, then to Toronto, Ontario. She did all kinds of odd jobs, sometimes imagining them as professions, but none felt right. Her attention was mostly placed on her home garden, boyfriends, friends, and family.

Her Returns started with a house fire. Thanks to a greedy Toronto real estate developer—arson—Simone lost almost everything she owned, including her late father's diaries, which she'd been saving to read when the loss was less fresh. After the fire, Mo's Returns took her to Florence, Italy, where she committed to study art restoration, a trade that perfectly marries her accrued talents. Art restoration was a path Simone had considered after undergrad, but wrote off, for the student loans she knew she'd have to take on, and the effort. It's hard work! But unafraid to scurry up and down the scaffolding to paint church ceilings, Mo's perfect for it. With an eye for color, an esteem for history, and a freak flag that's charming to the kinds of weirdos you meet in art and religion, I couldn't think of a better career for Simone, and she made it happen.

Simone has been experiencing depressions throughout her Returns. Usually the sun of the party, she's become antisocial bordering on agoraphobic. The last time I went to her apartment, we sat in the dark. Mo claims, "I've always been dark. What's new is that I'm tired too, so there's no hiding it." All the deaths Simone experienced young, which she felt but didn't fully process, she's now been going through. She says she's also been mourning the loss of her *jubilance*. (*Jouissance?* I text back. *yes. my wet . . . fire.* Our carefree, girly, fuck-me energy. Mine's waning too.)

When I met Mo, I was depressed—twenty-one and masking existential terror under vintage Chanel. Prissy, bitchy. Mo was this wild child. Juicy, messy, and mobile, she had layered affairs and an infectious levity—time for others. She was always horny and hungry for salami, baguettes, and brie. Mo could spend a whole day preparing for a dinner party, not because the food was complex. She'd take coffee breaks, reading breaks, nap, sex, and phone breaks. (Both her Sun and Rising are in slow-moving Pisces, and Montreal was so cheap at the time, one could really take her time.) There were inevitably one or two key ingredients Simone would have forgotten to buy. Too busy being charmingly lackadaisical to return to the store, she'd text a few guests to bring the missing ingredients. Often, we ended up with three different hunks of Parmesan. People would come to Mo's meals and stay for hours, late into the night, and sometimes the next morning, afternoon, and evening. Simone could corral a group of neuro-diverse near-strangers to chill. She called us "wizards."

I remember once, early in our friendship, Simone and I got coffee and then went grocery shopping together. Later, when we were hanging out in a small group, Simone recounted the tale of our day. It sounded epic! "And then," she storied, "all of these pears started tumbling and—" She couldn't stop laughing. It wasn't the day I had experienced. My day had been cold, stressful, same-old. Listening to Simone tell it (her audience rapt), I suddenly experienced it differently. The sky *had been* "a twisted shade of purple." And the story that Vito, the local grocery store owner, had told us *had been* "hilarious!"

When I moved to New York a couple years later (initially: because I thought Simone would be going too), I got my best friend's middle name—*Palma*—tattooed on my left wrist. This, to channel her courage, goofiness, humility, and everyday narrative creativity. This, before I understood the qualities I discerned in others must be in me too.

The night of that failed first and final photo shoot at La Mariposa, a few seasons into my own Saturn Return, Morgan had been late (coming home from school), Max had been drunk, and I had been 100 percent in the Real and unable to stop crying. Alicia, Miffany, and Nadezhda had taken control of the situation, modeling in their bedrooms and on our roof in interchangeable outfits, while I was on the phone for the first time in five years with my first boyfriend.

We had been together for four years—I lost my virginity to him—and, then, when I was Morgan's current age, I asked for openness. I wanted to feel other people inside of me. He said no then yes then maybe no yes maybe no no no. I hated that (I thought) it was up to him. So I cheated on him with three men. My third affair inspired me out of our relationship. The sex was as good as I knew it should be. We'd fuck all night, and wake up fucking. So fun! My first boyfriend was devastated—"emasculated," he said. He offered to give me a few grand to get out of town. (*We existed in a small community. He didn't want to have to see me.* Insert eyeroll emoji.) I was rationally apologetic, but heart-truly? No. It felt like a worse betrayal to apologize for something that was good for me. Sex—good sex, real sex, not the idea or image of it—offered the first glimmer of what I'd later experience as the Real. Immersive, intuitive, singular-knowing. Bliss! Here-nowness.

But now I understood, on that late January evening in Los Angeles, at twenty-eight years old, how I had been selfish. How at some point, determined to liberate myself from a claustrophobic labyrinth of inner/outer confusion, I had become ruthless. In the name of feminine empowerment, I had enacted an unapologetic slut. I would have done anything to become "myself," but I already had ideas of what that was, and that was the problem.

Ideas can cut up your Real. In the past, when faced with disappointment, I've pretended to be *too cool* cynical, when really I was giddy AF. I became a writer not because I genuinely aspired to be one, but because the first admirable women I met when I moved to New York wrote for a living. I've never felt happy to see my byline, because it's always felt like a lie—like when I replied to that high school "friend" who threatened me, "Of course I'm not gay."

Oh, the things we do to fit in! I've always hated reality TV, from the very first season of *Survivor*, which my whole grade-seven class obsessed over. I can't even overhear reality TV without feeling like I'm in a dentist chair. (I do love Ryan Trecartin's reality TV rips, though, but that's an article.) For decades, I lived my life like I dressed myself in guises that I saw on others and loved *on them*. Some of the styles suited me, no doubt, but any look is incomplete without a fullness of spirit. When you're in the Real, you can wear anything, and it becomes you, as gracious truth, your Supreme Being, is infinitely complimentary.

Now that I'd experienced it, I realized: if I was Real, my first boyfriend was too. But I'd treated him, because I didn't feel myself to be, like he wasn't Real. The night of the photo shoot, I called to apologize for living in fantasies I actuated without considering their repercussions for others. I saw how I'd been crashing through the world—which included him—as though my eyes were half-closed, my fingers in my ears, going "la la la la la la la la la." (I was horrified by all I must have missed along the way.) "It's okay," he told me. "It's true, you always seemed like you were striving to be elsewhere."

I had been restless most everywhere until, it seemed, this very moment. That night, on the fourth floor of La Mariposa, I was blissfully Earthbound. Gravity and Grace! Acutely perceiving little details—like the warble of Alicia's speaking insecurities, the grooves of Max's chest, and the fact that the exposed-brick wall I'd faced on so many mornings here was actually fake: a facade. That was funny.

I was calm, and felt overwhelmingly sweet, liberating *love*. BIG LOVE. Compassion like I'd learned to feel alone, meditating, and could feel in the company of a boy-lover (the root of the word *passion* is *pati*, as in to *endure, undergo, experience,* or *suffer*), but which, for whatever reason, I hadn't been able to feel in groups of people, and never around other women, except for Simone. Now letting this in—I couldn't stop crying. Grateful tears, mournful tears. I was alive. *This was Real.* And I was so happy—so, so, so happy—about what I was experiencing, except: What the fuck was this stranger doing in our home, shooting my beloveds as if for some lifestyle catalog? What had I done!

When Morgan came home, I cornered her in the bathroom.

"I need to talk," I said maybe for the first time in my whole life. ("We need to talk," I'd said to boy-lovers before. But I? Need? I tried to only have needs I could meet myself.) I told Morgan it felt like I'd eaten four grams of mushrooms but I'd only eaten a chicken salad.

Welcome to the Real World! Where furniture is multidimensional! See this chair? It was made from a tree. A Real living thing! Like you and me.

The awakening had been coming. I'd flickered into the Real in Morgan's bedroom, and every so often, walking around LA, I would step into It. This space of knowing where my heart, mind, and something more—some spirit sense—operated at the same time. When I had all the time in the world, and understood my place in It.

We're suspended in the sky! Four floors high. Below our feet are three strangers' homes and a basement, and then concrete, and maybe roots from nearby trees, and rocks and metals and ha ha ha I'm so dumb!

Out of It, before, I perceived the world as a blur, like what you see when you're running. Or it'd be partly obscured, like I was looking out from behind something, or through a frame—no peripheral, no turning back. I'm talking about decades of partial or total unreality. Hiding from the Real in movie theaters, behind the glamour of clothes, or in bed with a book. Escaping into drugs like boys. "La la la la la la la la la." I held my breath for fifteen years trying to get my gut as flat as that of a girl in a magazine, limiting the oxygen to my brain.

"Morgan," I said. "I've been seeing things. Like the other day, I was with Modesty"—a mutual friend of ours—"and she was talking about someone who had wronged her, and her top lip twitched so obviously, it was like a cartoon, like in slow-motion. Her anger was palpable as hurt. I recognized its texture, and it's the weirdest thing . . . My heart then, it beamed with love for her."

Morgan nodded.

"And Nadeem!" I exclaimed. He was this Washington-raised Afghan skater boy I'd been dating. "Sweet Nadeem at the end of our third date last week drove us back to his place without asking first. We hadn't done more than make out yet. And so I teased him. I was like, 'What are we doing here?' And I swear, Morgan, his head reeled from side to side, so fast, like a robot about to combust! He was like"—I was laughing now, mimicking Nadeem's shy manners—"'Oh uh well I uh uh uh uh I uh thought maybe uh.' And again, like with Modesty, I saw this as if in slow-motion, *and I felt him*. Have you ever experienced this?"

"No," Morgan said. "But I think I get it."

"I'm just like . . . I know that's me too. I know I'm a cartoon!"

Morgan looked transfixed. We all were longing for something like this. We talked about it constantly in our apartment: revelations, transformations. "I'm aggressively trying to heal!" was Morgan's punch line.

"Morgan—" I leaned in to her as my voice lowered to a guilty half whisper. "I made Nadeem like me. I made it happen, like this photo shoot, I made it happen. I'm afraid. I don't know what I'm doing, and I keep doing it! I imagine these things ... I always wanted to date a cute skater boy like him. It's like I make up these stories and characters, and then they become Real, but then I don't know what to do. And ..."

I was completely ignoring the photo shoot I was supposed to be directing. People kept asking for guidance, and I'd reply, "Just be yourself!" then look away.

Morgan was patient, in her college hoodie, makeup half ready to join the others in our shoot. "It sounds like there's an interplay between your imagination and reality?" she said. "And that's a gift, and maybe also scary?"

"It feels like a responsibility," I said. Suddenly I was so tired. I watched Morgan join the group for a few final poses in the kitchen, then I ordered the photo shoot over, and slept dreamlessly for many nights after.

Episode 07—"Bob"

I FIRST CAME TO KNOW of Amalia Ulman as an enigmatic young artist, a friend of friends, who made eerily graceful images that were novel with the potential to become fashionable. What she was making back then, circa 2012–13, was formal and impersonal. Loving the mystery, I followed her closely.

Over the course of a few months, in 2014, I watched Amalia's output on social media begin to change. Her face and body took center stage in a life that appeared to be styled according to lifestyle trends for a hyper-femme identity. She seemed to be branding herself alongside whatever trends were also selling: *kawaii* sweet, sugar baby x label whore, white girl–bad girl hip-hop looks, enlightened-health-guru vibes. The way she was doing this—it was believable. Every image she produced looked like she'd made it, bearing traces of her earlier aesthetic, while also seeming *basic*, in the way that people had started derisively coupling the word with this one: *bitch*. From my Internet voyeur position, it seemed that Ulman had chosen to trade in her high-art aspirations for the immediate gratification of transactional femininity, and this disturbed me, because a part of me wished I could do the same thing.

I've dabbled. Desperate for cash, I've tried "sugar babying." That's sex work veiled in mentorship, patronage, romance, and/or innocence. There's an app for it. I liked dressing the part, in snug cardigans and peach blush, but the privilege of my entitlement always kept me from taking it any further than a man paying for my dinner.

I couldn't fake it. I gagged into my latte when a rare-guitar dealer and former Rolling Stones tour manager claimed his backstage dealings were actually a "conceptual art performance." After googling the name on the credit card of another daddy, who claimed to be a lead writer on *The Colbert Report*, and finding no credits to the name, I ambushed our second date with Miffany, who, high as heaven, asked him the same invasive questions about *faith* and *feelings* she asks everyone, and Nadezhda, who mocked his replies. Dude paid for everything and sent me an e-mail the next day: "If you continue to keep company like that," he wrote, "I see nothing but ruin on your horizon."

My last *forever ewwww* sugar daddy date was with a "financial entrepreneur" who called me a car to the Glendale mall. There we had sushi as he told me about his plans to get into the movies ("It's like *Taken*, but the sex slaves all have special skills—think topless trampoliners."), about his twelve-year-old daughter ("The doctor I had take her measurements is predicting she'll be as tall and stacked as her mother, my ex-wife, five foot eleven, 36DD, and blond. I'm in trouble."), and finally, about the time he met Donald Trump ("He didn't want to shake my hand until I showed him the hand sanitizer I keep on me at all times.").

This pig-faced man kept calling me "Delicious," and I felt very righteous, because clearly he hadn't learned how to be psychic: I'd been glaring into his eyes thinking *you're vile, repugnant, idiotic,* and *pathetic* since we sat down. As our plates were being cleared, this loathsome character asked me if I'd like to go "to a motel nearby for a massage, but first—and I always ask this—I'd like us both to take showers separately using different bars of soap. I'm something of a germaphobe."

I stood up and said I'd rather not.

After calling me a car to the fake address I provided, he asked me to text him: "Once you're in the Uber, why you're not interested."

"I'll do it right here," I replied, emboldened by my recent consumption of lean protein and the crowd of witnesses in the restaurant. "Financial capitalism, the work you do, and the culture you promote are greedy and nearsighted, afflicting large populations of the nation, America, which you claim to adore, including your daughter, who I pray has an escape plan. You should leave her body alone. The world is changing, your ways are becoming irrelevant, and I think you know it. And the tassel on your left loafer is missing."

His pink face boiled crimson as he huffed all pouty like a toddler told no for the first time.

When I got home, the fridge at La Mariposa was filled with Moon Juice. Every shelf and drawer was stacked with pastel pink, mauve, green, cream, and gold milks; electric-blue and pink waters; cold brew with silver flakes; the lot. Store policy was to trash all products the night of the day they were made, even if they wouldn't technically expire for a few more days. Miffany was working there part-time and would bless our home with leftovers. I felt like a happy princess drinking pearl-infused strawberry-rose-probiotic-almond-whatever whatever. I *love* femme shit like this. *But*, I resolved to myself then, I'll go without if the only way to get the funds to afford it is entertaining male delusion.

When Ulman began posting square photos of her brand-new boob job, I lost it. If my list of financial priorities wasn't rent, food, debt, books, art, rent (it comes every month! like your period, ugh), I'd consider implants. (Big tits are one of my top turn-ons.) I called a friend who knew Amalia. "Is this real?" I asked him. "I don't know," he replied. "I haven't spoken to her in a while."

So I wrote Amalia a shy *hey, I was hoping you might like to talk?* She replied that she'd be happy to meet up soon. Sooner still, it came out that Amalia Ulman's covetable social media presence was an art performance about gender, attention economies, and belief production. (Several of the images she had posted, like the chest wrapped in post-surgery bandages, were appropriated from online forums.)

When we finally connected, a few months later, I was stunned by Amalia's composure. Unlike everyone else I'd met who was "Internet famous" or trying to be (her performance had awarded her a six-digit audience), Amalia wasn't caught up in any persona in person. She was attentive and sensitive, asking knowledgeable questions, but also goofy and funny—librarian manners meets clown-school mannerisms. I've listened to too much judgment in my day—persona pushers tend to attack those who risk threatening their facade, be they competitors, skeptics, or disbelievers. Amalia wasn't judgmental, but I did perceive that she was very perceptive to people's bullshit—delusion, ruthless ambition, vanity, cruelty, greed—and would do herself the service of avoiding any ego who might interrupt her positive flow.

I had a sense that Amalia and I spent our early lives similarly alienated but dealt with it in different ways. An only child, Amalia grew to relate to form, her craft, first and foremost. She carved out time for herself; she became an artist. Discerning in her friendships, Ami kept her circle so small, sometimes it was just a line between her and another, sometimes a dot. I spent a lot of my early life outside the house, at playgrounds and community centers, among dozens of elders and even more kids. As my parents worked overtime, I grew to observe. To clock points of likeness in others, even if they were sparse. I learned to fake it, to be that one thing we had in common. *Mirror/rorriM*. I adapted to the world around, learned to see from others' points of view, justified all—even ill—behavior with empathy, in order to not be alone.

This meant that, when I first met Amalia, I was in the second-to-last of a series of relationships with boys I wanted to be. They were free. Self-determined, cocky. Writers and artists. Amalia was more successful than all of them combined, and she was doing it making work that hit me on more levels of my being than I was used to experiencing simultaneously.

Amalia drove the same car my parents had throughout my childhood. I was ashamed of it then—this old, boxy Volvo, so "other" compared with the sleek new leases my friends' parents drove. "Embarrassing!!" I had screamed then. Real funny, I think now. My parents are eccentrics. When I was a teenager, we lived in a surreally normative neighborhood. My parents moved us there because the public schools were good. I remember my mom driving a few of my pristinely dressed friends around in our filthy old Volvo, talking about the SSRIs she and my dad were on like it was NBD. This was the early aughts, *it was common.* But I was mortified, just as I was when my mom would dance groovy rock 'n' roll style in the mall or my dad would joke about politicians getting anal probed while we were eating dinner.

Early in our relationship, Amalia invited me on a field trip. I'd just moved to LA in large part thanks to Ami, who had lent me her apartment for two weeks as a trial—that's when I met Nadezhda, agreed to sublet a bed in Mariposa, and "fell in love with" Lucien. When I saw Amalia's car, I knew I was home. Amalia drove us to Vernon. She, at twenty-six, had just gotten her license. I, then twenty-eight, still hadn't gotten mine, and like everything I hadn't yet done, it seemed insane. *Could I ever?!* Amalia put sneaky jazz piano on in the car like we were in a film noir. We were going to get a bird.

At the Polleria in Vernon, there were doves, chickens, a parakeet, and two pigeons. Amalia picked the pigeon with the classic coat. It was patterned like a business suit, I recognized then. Masculine and shady. His name would be Bob and Amalia would live and make art with him for almost two years—a pet. As an icon, under Amalia's wing, the pigeon came to represent a proletariat—homeless, commoners, scavengers—business-ing up in America. Class mobility. In China, I learned through Amalia, pigeons connote prestige; they're racing birds, winners.

Bob would fly around Amalia's Downtown LA high-rise office in custom-fit diapers. He was beautiful, with a shimmery neck like my great-aunt's fire-opal ring I always wore. Bob became the star of Amalia's art, drawn like a Picasso dove, collaged as memes, a guardian angel to her pregnant Mary. Now my experience of cities is forever changed, as Amalia changed what it means to see a pigeon.

I was raised with the language virus: *You can be anything you want to be.* Wishful public-school teachers, my Republican stay-at-home grandmother, and TV, magazines, and advertisers constantly repeated this promise to me. They inspired my wide-eyed *want want want*, while imaging none but a few options and calling it *everything*, and offering almost no counsel on *how* to get things done. Girls are lied to. We can be whatever we are, but it's not going to be easy. We can do whatever we want, but we won't necessarily be rewarded for it by the powers that be. As girls in this world, we're raised around so many ideas, and even more images, of what we should want to be that it can be hard to sort out what's true for you.

My creativity became bound to fashion: *If I just put on this outfit, I can become the person with the life it signifies.* Amalia had an amazing closet, but she was also so accomplished, it mystified me. I'd been a straight-A student, but I had no idea how to get from point A to B to car and career and back to art.

Driving with Amalia to buy Bob for ten dollars transformed me. This was when I learned: *We* can *do anything.* There were so many options I'd never considered, so organized was my mind by norms. There's a look to consciousness expanding. The scene around you will intensify or deepen as you lighten and open. In the car, driving home from the Polleria, Bob cooing in the back seat, jazz still bopping, the city lights were brighter, and the drive flowed smoother, or maybe I was just alert, finally noticing our current in a state of all-too-rare-for-me relaxed receptivity.

Amalia opened my mind to possibility. What would I do if money wasn't part of the equation? Where would I be if I'd never been told that my worldviews were "unrealistic," and believed it? If I hadn't read the Great Western Man canon and tried to identify? Even though I really didn't—war seemed to me a horrible hoax to give men's lives meaning. Look, we're heroes! We conquered a conflict we started. And Kant versus Hegel? Or the mind/body binary? Nature versus nurture? What strange oppositions. Obviously, it's all functioning simultaneously, enmeshed, there's no me that's not you. And the mind can think any which way and find proof of its ideation in the world. The world is so complex.

If you could do *anything*, what would it be? After the drive to pick up Bob, I started asking myself this question. Most of the ideas I came up with were dust, I let them blow away. One image that lingered was of a community center—a special educational retreat, like Professor X's Mutant Academy, where my favorite freaks could train, trade, rest, and play. It would be slightly off-center, with water for swimming, gardens, animals, studios, and multiple kitchens.

La Mariposa was broke. A few of us were poor, with families who were lower class or refused to support us. In America, this is dangerous. Not having money makes you a target. You're mailed high-interest credit card offers weekly. If you get sick or hurt and end up in the hospital, you're liable to leave with tens of thousands in debt or more. Quality fresh foods are vital, but they're harder to find in lower-income neighborhoods than high-fructose corn syrup is, which poisons the treats we crave to make ourselves feel better; candy abounds in our corner of LA. Then there's the illnesses of stress: how fear, scarcity, and shame, imagined failure, infect the body. The dark side of the Dream.

We were also cute and smart, though—what my father, who hates American power games, calls "the other 1 percent." Attractive, intelligent, and savvy enough to scale class brackets, we could probably, if we really wanted to, achieve: fame and/ or money, illusions of safety, US success! Capitalizing on our blessings—like our curiosity to learn, our interest in cultivating our talents, and our juicy youth—could spoil them though. Easy come, easy go. Our youth would soon. Beauty is fickle. And God leaves the room when you sell out; it just happens, sorry.

Sometimes we wished we didn't know better. We wished we could *just do it*. Package our work and selves into market-ready forms, join in, and *win*. But something inside us refuses to reinforce a system that demands that *we* appeal to *it*, while *it* demonstrates little to no awareness or interest in who we really are and will probably fuck us over. But there's got to be another way.

The way most of our peers sought success was through music, fashion, cool, youth, branding. Another way was through "art." The art world has money. "It's money games for plastic faces," my friend Tracy, an artist I met after an opening and whose paintings sell for $15K, says.

We knew art kids who had mansions. Usually, these kids were the sons of preexisting wealth who knew how to work the system, but we knew how to watch them. There are enough stories of under- and middle-class "artists" "making it" for people to believe and pursue the Dream. The problem with the Dream is it's not so dreamy in reality. It's more like Monopoly or Risk than the fantasies I want to make Real.

"Make more red paintings!" Tracy's first Los Angeles gallerist demanded. "And never put words in. Words don't sell."

My first boyfriend used game theory to win $300K playing online poker in 2008. Excited by the prospect of making money, I tried to learn, but found theory irksome. *Assuming your opponent is working for his own best interest as a rationally intelligent decision-maker in a made-up system? And having to behave the same?* Apparently, modern economics and politics are founded in the same theory.

I always hated games like Monopoly and Risk. I remember

more than once throwing these boards across a yard, delighted to see their miniature war machines and buildings disappear into flowers and grass. At recess in grade five, I convinced half the student body to play my way every day. We played truth or dare, seven minutes in heaven, and make-believe. We all kissed and hugged and wrote and told stories about our innermost desires. "I've never met a more sexually charged grade-five cohort!" Mme. Partridge exclaimed. No one ever ratted me out as our perverted leader. Mousy, quiet, and petite, I get away with a lot.

The residents of La Mariposa are ambitious like me. We want revolutions of popular consciousness (spiritual, queer, Aquarian Aging), as well as alterations to our economic systems (redistributions of wealth and new definitions of it based on *what we really value*, like love and longevity). Some of us, like Nadezhda, are more materialist. She studies machinery, systems, and code. Morgan studies her body: nutrition, addiction, and fitness. Max is Mephistophelian and many other modes of mythic (the canons within!), while Miffany intuitively nurtures. I was astounded by Alicia's intimate understanding of cycles of attachment, abuse, and trauma, especially with regard to sensual heterosexual dynamics and American racial politics. I learned so much. And most of this was happening in the privacy of our home.

I wanted to publicize La Mariposa's knowledge and our dreams, our insecure reality and alternative visions. I was—and still am—convinced they're common. *Maybe we could catalyze a movement?* But the means I sought to make our dreams known were too mixed up in the Dream. To be seen, moneyed, on screen.

After I broke the contract, I had to scramble for money. I didn't know what to do, so I made an appointment with a professional witch. Sylvia worked out of a Los Feliz Craftsman house, where she lived with a roommate and three cats. She usually charged a minimum of a hundred bones for her services, but in order to showcase a new program—a three-month-long mentorship that promised *prosperity*—she was taking free meetings with prospective mentees.

When I arrived, I realized I was wasting her time. Mentorship cost three grand. I'd walked the hour from Koreatown to Sylvia's place to talk about my lack of funds. When it became clear I didn't have the resources to hire her, Sylvia suggested I "put it on a credit card!" This made me feel less guilty for taking the free meeting; we each had our own schemes.

I'm not sure how it came out, these things just do around me, but sometime during our meeting Sylvia told me she used to do sex work. I told her I was considering sugar babying again, but that I only wanted to do it if I could be a sacred prostitute, like the Sumerian goddess Inanna. Sexual healing, and respected for it.

"Do you know what an egregore is?" Sylvia replied.

I shook my head, excited by a new word.

"An egregore," Sylvia explained, "is a spiritual entity that is created through the collective thoughts and ritual participation of groups of people throughout time. Initially, the egregore is a thought form, an idea. It's created from and by the human mind. How it got there in the first place is another question, one that gets at the heart of the occult, so perhaps it's a bit much to go into now, but as people connect to this spirit, as we worship, paint pictures, whisper chants, write hymns, and contemplate and fetishize and pray to it, this spirit, or idea, becomes Real. It becomes its own thing, which then starts to influence and inform the people who interact with it, and even people who don't, who are just in proximity to it."

Sylvia's two examples of egregores were the Whore and Jesus Christ.

"Even if there was a historical Jesus," she said, "what Jesus Christ is now is far beyond what the man was then. He's an abstraction, an archetype, and . . . he's Real. Above and beyond how people conceive of him, he exists independently of the Church, of any single person or religion, exerting influence all over the world."

Sylvia's point was that no matter how mindfully I went into sex work, I would be contending with millions upon millions of people's ideas (including my own) of what a whore is. It's hard not to be influenced by this. Collective (un)consciousness. We may think we're just putting on the uniform of a job we can then take off, but the codes of these ancient ways are powerful—they'll seep in, become us.

The idea of the egregore helped me understand why I had killed our reality show contract. Why, as soon as the lark became real, I developed a fearsome allergy to visibility. I knew, no matter how smart we tried to play it, how our show—how we—would be received. *Pretty Young Things, Repeat After Me, I Said Na Na Na (Na Na Na) Na Na Na Na Na.* Girl forms aren't taken seriously. That's what the branding agency was paying for. All-girl sleepovers. Shots of us getting dressed up. Most people hate-watch TV. And reality TV!? I'd always hated it! Why had I thought to make this show in the first place? Because everyone I told the story of my life to told me to. *In Los Angeles.*

I had been, not for the first time, organizing my life according to norms. I had embarked to fulfill expectations and desires that were not only not my own, but also counter to my own expressed interests. But this was worse than ever before, because I would have been taking five young friends along with me!

Episode 08—"Fizzy ill logic and taut! oh law gee"

We live at a rare evolutionary turning point yet our attitudes and ideologies have not caught up.

We are still too programmed by the oldworld psychology of failure, too hobbled by guilt and shame and self-doubt, too scarred by eons of suffering and privation to fully appreciate the meaning of our New Age.

—FM-2030, *Up-Wingers* (1973)

"I FEEL LIKE I'M TRAPPED behind glass," Morgan said, miming a tight wall around her with her hands. "It's like an aquarium. I'm in this glass box and I can see you all on the other side and I want to join, but I can't break through."

I hadn't seen Morgan in months. After we decided we

wouldn't make TV together, she had deferred her studies in the middle of winter semester and retreated to her family home in the Bay. It was summer now, and I'd agreed to take care of two cats who belonged to one of my mom's friends for three weeks in Oakland. Albert was athletic and mischievous. Nabokov was neurotic; I had to give him kitty Prozac every other day. I was staying close enough to Morgan's home for her to drive over one afternoon.

Morgan's anxiety had been one of many reasons why I killed the deal. During our one-on-one interview, it had become clear to me how unclear she was within herself. It was like looking in a rearview mirror. Morgan behaved like I had at her age: dysphoric anxiety, splitting personalities. She questioned everything—brilliant lines of thinking, but too many, simultaneously. She'd get lost trying to connect It All, then panic under uncertainty.

Back in the Bay, Morgan was in treatment at her parents' behest. She insisted to her fifth doctor, "I don't have an eating disorder, I have an anxiety disorder that manifests as an eating and exercise disorder." She seemed great to me, except that she was ninety pounds.

We went on a pilgrimage to our favorite American sanctuary: the grocery store. This one was an independently owned mega health food store, like Whole Foods before Whole Foods, a hippie haven in Oakland. There we bought French and Spanish cheeses, local tomatoes, cucumbers, lemons and limes, cumin, pistachios, fresh figs, purple yams, dinosaur kale, olives, sardines, two varieties of cantaloupe, and jackfruit from Mexico.

We took our lot back to the house where I was cat-sitting and prepared to eat.

Jackfruit tastes like cotton candy. It's got a hard shell and little pods of frothy flesh you have to excavate from tight compartments of what feels like cartilage. We gave up using cutlery and dug in with our fingers—my nail beds stayed sticky all afternoon.

Communal meals were common at La Mariposa when Morgan and Miffany lived there. The first I witnessed was pupusas with spicy slaw served out of a plastic bag. Morgan liked to roll homemade sushi. Her vegan "ice cream" consisted of frozen bananas and cocoa powder blended in a food processor. Ice cream–like for about three minutes before it melted flat—she'd urge us to eat it fast. Morgan must've been 115 fit pounds when we first met. She'd talk about her anorexic past and her oral fixation as a problem, but I didn't take it that seriously because she seemed so *perfectly* healthy, and every femme I knew had food control issues.

But then I shadowed Morgan on an errand run around town. I had just start researching our show. "Driving in LA makes me nervous," Morgan said. "So I chew gum." She had thirty packs in the compartment between our safety-belt locks, and more in the glove box. Chewing to her manic heartbeat, whenever the wad in her mouth became too stiff, she'd stick it onto her steering wheel before popping more minty elastic into her mouth. By the end of our forty-minute drive, Morgan's wheel was covered in white mounds like the peaks of the San Gabriel Mountains.

It's unclear what caused Morgan's anxiety disorder. There

was a migration from Colombia to California, but Morgan was barely old enough to remember, she remarked, as she chopped up more cucumbers than could fit in either of our stomachs.

"But maybe that's the issue!" she continued. "They say the early years set you up. If you're not held enough, or looked at with love, it can fuck you up." She also had a work-hard father, a self-made success, who expected a lot from her. "But he's also—and Mom—they're really great," she countered. "Or they did their best. I know I'm blessed. I should be grateful. Maybe I'm spoiled. Sometimes I think I'm stupid. Or it's like what we always used to talk about in Alicia's room: The world's changing, we're all leveling up at the same time, but it's hard. I have a hard time keeping up."

"You're only twenty-two," I said. "You don't need to have it all figured out already."

"I know, I know," Morgan said. "But there's this pressure, like only the prodigies matter. You should be famous by twenty-three. But also, I don't believe that—my heroes got good when they were older. Damn. I don't know!" She laughed.

By the end of our meal, after presenting dozens of hypotheses as to what was wrong with her, Morgan came to the only natural conclusion, with which I concurred: *A spiritual plague infects our society and culture. We aren't the only sufferers.*

That summer, Tracy made a beautiful painting of a rose garden. I was visiting her studio often, avoiding my personal life. Tracy was a friend of my friend Susan's friend. I liked being around her because she was honest, older, sober, and believed in magic.

The canvas was the size of the wall. Pink-red roses set against LA's blue sky. I saw it in her studio one week, and then the next week: it was half-covered in black paint.

"It's the view outside the window from my therapist's office," Tracy explained. She had been attending therapy every day, trading paintings for the service because she, like me, currently had very little money. Vertical blinds, represented by painted-black rough cuts of canvas, blocked the view of the rose garden I'd loved the week before. The garden had had me breathing easy, and now I felt trapped, angry, even, at Tracy for shutting us out.

I also understood. I know what it's like to feel as though the world—the beautiful and the Real—is inaccessible to you, and yet *right there*. There were nights in New York I screamed for escape, convinced I was in prison because an activist family friend in Egypt was, with no expectation of release, and this was skewered all over the news—twenty-four hours, and fake fake fake. I was writing journalism at the time, and knew how it went. An article was published in *W* under my name, but I hadn't written half of it. It was as if no one had. The writing was that which was absent of meaning: a product. I was learning so much about "the real world"—the business of media, encounters with power, et cetera—that I went crazy, because I hadn't yet learned to cultivate the stillness you need to process it all. I lived voraciously, lonely and hungry for information. I'd moved to this new country alone, never stopping to think, *That's kinda crazy*, maybe because I feared falling like Wile E. Coyote when he realizes he's walking on air. A year into this mental state, all I could hear 24/7 was the siren of anxiety.

You have to learn to simultaneously see yourself from without, while feeling from deep within. Or that's how I've saved myself. When I feel my heart surge, I zoom out with my eyes closed and watch my life's movie—which is always comical, even at its most tragic.

Morgan and Tracy are perfect to me. Creative, inquisitive, and novel. Perfect because I don't see their suffering—not even its side effects, like their selfish agoraphobia or infectious anger—as part of them. They've just caught a disease, like the best of us. The sensitive ones.

I want to heal us. It's delusional maybe, my disease. I want to remove the black blinds from Tracy's garden, have Simone restore the growth beneath, and then we'll all drink iced tea under weeping willows. Morgan will join. I'll have lifted the top off her aquarium, and called out from above for her to hear: "Don't you see, Morgan? You're a mutant, a talent, so special and alive. You can breathe underwater! Look how long you've survived." Cynical Susan will join us too, laughing her most graceful, childish giggle, having made a meal for all, reluctant mother that she is. And our Canadian friend Kimia—she'll be clementine, lilac, and gold, unburdened by the bruising purples I often see stalking her soul.

Once when I was real lost—delirious, anxious, dumb with evil thoughts—I painted Kimia. I'd just bought my first paint set, and I'd just seen her for the first time since we had both left New York and lost touch. I laid out my new paints and without judgment or expectation blotted and brushed my vision of Kimia: dark tides lurking violet and cream of peach. I hadn't been able to cry since she told me she thought she was dying, the week before, when I'd seen her in Montreal. "My head is shrinking," Kimia had said, and it was true—her eye sockets looked as though someone had punched into wet clay, and her skull was at least 12 percent smaller than I remembered, as if fired in a kiln. "*Don't tell anyone,*" Kimia had made me promise. "I'm going to go to the doctor but only when I'm done." She was in the middle of writing a screenplay she'd sold on spec. Her apartment felt like my bipolar grandmother's in the midst of a manic episode, when the air would shake, rustling her notes-to-self, and the trash littered everywhere, spooking all other life out. In a few strokes of paint, I was bawling. Thank God I couldn't see the canvas through my own home aquarium's worth of tears. My first painting! It was ugly, I tossed it, then I felt so light.

I wish writing felt less like revenge on the world. My first drafts are furious and petty. I delete whole chapters that critique the culture industry, and most of what I've written about Lucien. Then I turn my attention to what I'd ideally prefer to write about, like my friends. I'd like to write about us on a series of grand adventures, rather than homebound and depressed or anxious, but I'm not flexible enough in my creativity yet. I move through text as if lost in a cartoon jungle, machete in hand, guiltily cutting down foliage, hoping that my path of ruin leads, eventually, to a natural clearing, to safety and freedom.

Tracy says my vengeance is good: "That's a lot of what art is—*resistance*."

"No one out there wants us loving ourselves," I've heard Alicia say more than once.

For years, I hated that I read and wrote because it felt like evidence of my inability to connect. When I left a party because I was anxious, the book was the fallback, not the choice. I tried making writing—my job: arts journalism—less lonely by only writing about what I love for an imagined audience of those I love, but what I made was never as beautiful as the reality it reached toward. The writing was like the bird your cat mauls dead and delivers to your bedside with a pleased, evil look on her face. But eventually, by doing it, and doing it, and doing it more, reading and writing delivered bouts of transcendence. (I imagine this happens with anything you study long enough.) Learning its components, its infinite resonances and limits, words became the material of the world, and now and then: I could rewrite it. Make believe my Real. Edit, change, surrender. God comes through. Fingers moving without deliberate intention: that's the best writing.

When I got us caught in the reality show deal, I was still reveling in fantasies. My writing was like advertising, beautifully crafted received ideas projected onto reality. I was deep into astrology, New Ageisms, and Lucien, more Real obsessions, at least, than my previous year's—science fiction, romances with known con men, and a conviction that I alone could bring about the dissolution of capitalism from the confines of my bedroom.

"*That's* what you should write about," Susan and Kimia, two of my adopted (not that they consented) mentors, were always telling me. *That* was always after I'd tell them a real-life story, like how I treated the yeast infection I got from using a zucchini as a dildo (I was desperate!) with a clove of garlic and a little organic yogurt.

"Get out of the stars, Fi," Kimia kept advising, while seeing me struggle on Earth. Neglecting realities like the body, I was always getting sick and ending up in crappy emergency-care clinics I couldn't afford.

At the exact midway point—the peak, as they say—of my Saturn Return, I was in Oaxaca City for an artist residency. There I met a young woman named Teresa, half Oaxacan, half New York Jew. Teresa's mother was from Juchitán de Zaragoza, part of the Isthmus of Tehuantepec region of the postcolonial state. Thanks to its mountainous and therefore isolationist topography, the region's indigenous cultures have managed to maintain something of their unique history even after Spanish colonialism and US imperialism. Hundreds of local languages are still spoken around Oaxaca. In her mother's culture, Teresa told me, women are revered. They're responsible for making the main export, this beautiful embellished clothing, a regional craft, like what Frida Kahlo wore.

Juchiteca women are "tall, broad, expressive, and in charge," Teresa told me, "and there are also, in their culture, boy-girls, beloved femme men, kinda trans, but not—it's a fluctuating identity they call 'muxe.'" Some muxe present as women their whole lives, dating men, while others flow in and out of the feminine.

Teresa is superfemme, like Mama Matrix most mysterious. Curvy and curly-maned, she salsas snapping her hips and heels like she could a neck. She also, when I met her, was twenty-five and experiencing dysphoric depressions and anxiety. Teresa had just moved back to Oaxaca from Texas and New York to "recover" and "reset." It seemed like a majority of my girlfriends were doing this: Miffany, Clara, and Morgan were; I had the year before; and Alicia and Susan would the next year. We retreated and dropped out, to read, smoke, introspect, and feel closer to being safe, or invisible.

In college, Teresa told me, she once tried to be a sidewalk. Or, she decided she *was* the sidewalk. Being steady as concrete seemed wiser to her than rushing between classes during finals. She lay down, stiff as the ground in winter, on her favorite spot in the quad, where the afternoon light shimmered golden, next to an old oak whose bark reminded her of her father's beard. She got still—very, very still—still as stone, and she *was stone*, so of course she didn't hear her peers when they asked her what was up. Nor could she hear the dean when he asked her to move, and when her friends Hollis and Sean picked her up and carried her back to her dorm, she didn't soften, but rather stayed steady, steady stiff. They called that a depression. It seemed perfectly sensible to me. Hilarious, even though I know it must've been painful for Teresa.

I wish they hadn't medicated her. I wish I'd met people like Teresa and those of La Mariposa when I was younger. It would've saved me a lot of time and anguish; I thought I was crazy too.

When I was college-age, my party-happy friends would tell me, "Get out of your head," and "Think less." "You're neurotic." "Just do you, girl," they'd say.

"But I don't know what that means!!" I'd exclaim.

Then there were the brainy peers, intellectual-identified types, like my boyfriend at the time, who seemed to judge my vacuity. I like feeling empty. Like nothing. Receptive and worldly. Open to being filled up. I also love surface. Glamour. Beauty. Fashion. It'll be laughably anachronistic soon to think emptiness and surface and depth and intelligence are at odds.

I witnessed four panic attacks during my stay at La Mariposa. Four different souls willing themselves free from prisons of ego, trauma, debt, and fantasy. Five if you count me.

Joelle had just lost her job. Her best friend, Darya, had moved into Morgan's room after she left for the Bay, so Joelle came over to feel less crazy. Joelle's a delicate creature. She likes a set schedule and a steady paycheck, the security of "a real job," ideas Darya (who's an actress) and I have never entertained. It was midafternoon on a weekday. Darya suggested she and Joelle smoke a little weed to relax. I tuned in when the paramedics

busted in. Two young jocks, hate-fuckably built, were respond-
ing to a call of, "I'm dying!" Joelle, in a panic, had locked herself
in Darya's bathroom and called 911. It'd been almost an hour
since she called, two since they smoked the roach, but the bone-
heads put it all on the drugs.

"Make it stooooop," Joelle said. Her naked torso flailed as if
possessed. She was in Darya's bed looking like Regan MacNeil
in *The Exorcist*, with pallid, sweaty skin, green around the edges.

"Have you girls been smoking marijuana?" one of the medics asked.

Darya explained it'd been a mellow indica, hours ago. Meanwhile Joelle whined, "No, no, no. Make them go, make this stop,
I'm sorry, no."

Darya covered Joelle's bare chest. We rubbed her back with
open palms and I made my breath audibly oceanic, a trick I had
learned from Simone five years earlier, when our friend Phillip,
whose estranged mother had just died, tripped as if to hell to
find her. Simone had lured him back to our Montreal apartment
with her double-Piscean ocean breath.

"It's all in your head, sweetie," one of the medics (they really
were indistinguishable) said.

"We see this all the time."

"It's a bad strain, they're very common."

*Right, it's our state-regulated top-shelf medicinal marijuana
that's bad*, Darya mouthed back. We both knew what it was—a
panic attack. Classic.

"Tell her it's just in her head."

"It's just the drugs."

"We see this at least twice a week."

(I knew it was an epidemic! Anxiety is rampant, and bro-holes are getting paid to come into our homes to tell us it's not Real.)

The paramedics' cocky incompetence was only increasing Joelle's hyperventilating.

"You should go," Darya commanded, and the men walked away, convinced of their authority.

We made Joelle tea, got her in the shower, and then she took a nap. Thirty minutes later, she was present again.

"I've never had that happen," Joelle said.

She told us she was embarrassed. I replied she shouldn't be. In fact, a guilty part of me was relieved. Right before the medics stomped in, I had been fire-breathing in my room, trying to tame my own crazy-angry madness. It was a new moon, rent was due soon, and I felt trapped between an empty checking account and a thick uterine lining. Joelle looked light, almost radiant. Her anxious sweat had chilled to a glow. We hugged, and Joelle went home. The emptiness she left me with reminded me of the feeling I had after painting Kimia. Sometimes the tensions build and build and build, nations of toxic thoughts populate your assumed solitude; a claustrophobia inside your own skin, *stressed the fuck out*. The body is wise though. It'll make change happen, even if it's with a fit. Anything to clear the cache. The sensitive ones, I've noticed, tend to implode. It's Lucien curled in on himself crying onto my floor. It's Alicia wearing a mask of cool togetherness so no one will be burdened by her unraveling insides.

Alicia and I spent a lot of time talking about "healing." Except for Max, whose performative self-destructive rock-star habits kind of worked for him, all the residents of La Mariposa thought they needed "healing." Nadezhda sought to heal sexual trauma so she could experience penetrative sex again (a PTSD pussy will go on lockdown, and bar entry like a safe). Miffany sought to heal her relationship to God and "the gaze," and Morgan to stillness (she wanted to sit and make things, but could only find the courage to run, bike, and move), while Alicia wanted to not want—after the littlest conflict with the one she loved—"to go out and suck twenty cocks." *Ha ha.* I could relate. She also wanted a career—the confidence to work in the Real World. We didn't get it. How did people do it?

I loved listening to Alicia. I remember being intimidated, before I met her, by her persona, her social media and party presence; immaculate, potent, aggressive. At home, in sweats, she was soft and intelligent. She could quote Ren and Stimpy, Kanye, and William Blake in swift succession. Her half-a-room was a cocoon of fuck-me heels, shredded clothes like fallen armor, ruby-red blankets, and books: *Urban Tantra*, *Weetzie Bat*.

I remember one Sunday, listening to Alicia talk about her family history. I was on the floor, she was on her bed, makeup-free in sweats. With her shaved eyebrows, incisive gaze, and regal posture, she looked like a Sphinx—I kept getting goose bumps.

"I recently realized I'm very prideful," Alicia said. I'd just asked, "What's new?"

"When I really need help," she continued, "I keep to myself. I get determined to do it all on my own, too fearful to reach out. And that's when I've gotten really sick."

Sick like so many of us are. We get dim. The world around us spins. It feels like we're running for our lives when we're sitting still. We self-medicate with whatever's near: media, carbs, sex, drugs, jobs. Escapism. We feel worse. Deserving of it. Or we pretend it's all good. We strive and strive and strive toward goals we're indifferent to. Act so fabulous people get jealous of us. Validation. More escapism. Sleep twelve hours a day, or never. Reality gets dreamy, and we—vacant, numb, or meaningfully volatile, entertained—watch it stream. Irresponsible. Pretending not to care safeguards us from real feelings. Complaining is almost like doing. It's all their fault. Or it's all ours. We suck. Might as well 💀 💀 💀. We cut for release. Walk around screaming inside. Hurt ones we love. Deny, deny. Some of us control the trap we feel we're in by shaking it up. Our snow globe's in a flurry; agitation, glamour, distraction. Or we get very, very still. Hold our breath. Play dead.

It didn't occur to me to ask what Alicia meant by "sick." It's all around us. Instead, I asked, "What helped?"

"I started looking to my ancestry," Alicia replied. "From the origins of my name to my parents', grandparents', and *tías'* lives, family secrets and generational struggles. I always made a point of listening to family stories, so I won't make the same mistakes, so they didn't go through it for nothing."

Alicia's mother's father, I learned, is from the Philippines. Her mother's mother was from Tennessee. She was black. He worked in asparagus fields. She waitressed at a diner. They met in California in the late 1930s and had five kids.

"There was a lot of violence around," Alicia said. "My mom's mom was taken away by the cops once when my mom was a girl. No one explained why, they just showed up. My grandma was gone for two years for mental shit. Nobody knows what she was diagnosed with, but she came back with no teeth, and she didn't talk much after that. I know that was a huge event for my mom. More shit happened too. It's just a lot of trauma. A lot of pain. I just want to understand. I really would like to know what the hell I'm here for besides watching all these people I care about be sad about things they should not have to be sad for."

That's the plaguing question.

"Maybe I'm so obsessed with this history stuff," Alicia continued, "because if I can break through and do things differently, then others can too, and then collectively . . ."

In my fantasies, I'm the leader of an interstellar feminine rebellion. "Buddhist, psychedelic, green, feminist culture," my hippie character croons. "It'll save the world, man." Trees are our allies. I communicate with them. Wiser than men, one touch of a trunk and I'm Real again. Of course trees are wise—staying in one place teaches you a lot. Being broke, I do this often. I'll set myself up at a fancy hotel pool ("My boyfriend's staying here"—I relish lying to big business), or at a public park, a library, a café, Venice Beach, and I watch. The blocks around MacArthur Park are as wild as a Glendale mall or Beverly Hills or South-Central. I like watching humans move, the paces of different classes and our clothing styles. (You know why high fashion's obsessed with derelict chic? Hobo style? It's because the homeless wear their God-given wares like they don't give a fuck. That's what "cool" is in fashion. Disaffection.) Most of us out here in America, I've learned from my neighborhood watch, are bent on survival. In Santa Monica, survival is clothed in yoga tights—all the kept white women. Around MacArthur Park, we depend on social services, camaraderie, God, and other drugs.

Trees apparently communicate underground. Through root networks, they share news of water sources and viruses. The Internet runs like roots underground too. My father, a computer engineer (he builds the hardware the Internet runs on), explained this to me once. After that, I started fantasizing about digging up and sawing through the cables our interconnection depends on.

I've loved the Internet. Without it, I wouldn't have met La Mariposa or Susan, Kimia, Ana, Clara, Amalia, Asher, Alexa, Stefan, or Misty. The Internet delivered me my interiority: multivalence, confidence. It was my playground, a training ground. Circa 2012–15, my full-immersion years, I loved the Internet like my life depended on it. Now I'm not suggesting we break up, more like it's time to transition to an open relationship.

This is in part what I wanted our reality show to be about. I saw how my new Mariposa friends were, like I'd been, so committed to being online. We spent years cuddled up in bed with it, like the first spell of romance. But the magic of the medium we loved, I was convinced, had expired, become rotten, poisoned by corporate interests and competitive language viruses (like "likes"). Said another way: Our souls had outgrown it. If we stayed in as we'd been, we'd get sick. Sicker than we've been.

Episode 09—"Angels Flight"

I LOVE LOS ANGELES. I walk it convinced I am the place. I am the parched palms. I am the Bank of America sign, sun-bleached pink. I am every storefront psychic. I am homeless, Hills rich, and delusional. I'm a faithless aspiring actress. I'm sex on the beach. Dogtown, Downtown, *Blade*. I am longing, I am meth, I am porn and a press pass. I'm the Boomer in a blue Mustang blasting the *Indiana Jones* theme song on a residential street in Hollywood, and I'm the guy in a pearl minivan who jerked off as I gave him directions to the Beverly Center. I am Dennis Hopper, Angelyne, Thom Andersen, Jaden Smith, and Norma Jean Almodovar, LAPD's finest. I am my retro drug dealer, Justin Moonbeam, and his two fat cats, Raymond and Chandler. I'm fresh-cut pastel flowers perennial at the Beverly Hills Hotel. I'm missing the bus that only comes every forty minutes. I'm

parasols in Chinatown, a Spanish church service, a plastic sur-
geon, a power lesbian, and the energy healer who recommended
I read Walt Whitman. Nihilism, Zen wisdom, Café Gratitude,
jacaranda, sunshine, and secrets. I am screenwriting at Intelli-
gentsia and introduced as an intellectual as if that's novel. I'm a
true story. I can't write fiction.

I am love.

Nowhere have I felt so happy to have stereotypes confirmed.
When the unsurprising surprises, I think, *That's love*. Every day
delightful. When the sorrow is meaningful. I love the raggedy
drunk I bought mermaid art from on the Venice Beach board-
walk. I love cruising skater boys, the folds of their socks. I love
hiking as a slightly inclined walk and girls doing it in full faces of
makeup. I love hippie bumper stickers. I love grocery stores with
valet. I love being surrounded by my friends! Celebrities, I grew
up watching you. Screens and magazines were my extended
family. Tim Robbins smiling at me from his beach cruiser.
Bruce Willis's girls. Willie Nelson's son. Jennifer Aniston. Of
course I feel at home in LA. Everyone's lit like a star under our
sun. Even our trees look like stars! Bursts precariously swaying
on a thin shoot or mopped atop a thick pineapple trunk. Lucien
calls it Hell A. He compares rush-hour freeways to clogged ar-
teries. Heart attacks and heartbreak.

My mom said this of baby shit: that it smells almost sweet
when it's from your own born. I would have been a fifth-
generation Californian if my parents hadn't left LA with me
eight months in utero. Is that why the sight of blond surfer
locks and that violet blue my parents painted their garage

door—which made no sense in Ontario, but then, when I moved here, I saw it everywhere—why these tones wow me so? Why I walk around this town crying? Salty tears watering my feared-barren heart to blossom. I love the *love loves to love love* graffiti that spoils our city. It wouldn't be all over the place if we didn't need it, I know that. LA is dark. A portal to the underworld. Full of rapists and liars. Neptune's net.

The other day, in his rented Porsche, my millionaire friend Henry Gaylord-Cohen said, "This city makes no sense!" As in, it's not a grid. He lives in New York. We kept getting lost. Los Angeles is built in pockets, bursts, and loops. To me, that makes perfect sense. *Everything makes sense here*, I wrote my friend Misty, who replied, *Of course*. We find calm in the chaotic, sprawling, conspiratorial, the fake and natural beauty, the insanity and inanity of this place. It's good to have your outsides reflect your insides.

The tragedy of my love for Los Angeles is that I might not be able to stay. I'm not rich enough to live like the rich here; in hills or by water, health insured, massaged, lemon trees on my property. Nor do I have the grounded community that could ease the stress of poverty.

It's weird when you realize you're living history. That you're part of a demographic, a trend, socioeconomic fuckery. My aspirational millennial cohort is financially fucked, the reports all say, and I still can't help but take it personally.

I feel shame—like I'm a loser—because I can't seem to make

money, or at least not ethically. Every time I follow the means offered to me, it's deadly. Like selling kids things they don't need, breeding insecurity; working for mass-market magazines. Or sucking off rich men; validating their cons. My relationship to money is sickness. It's a slow slug to the chest, pinched shoulders, shortness of breath. It's feeling like a frightened mouse who keeps getting run over by steroid-fattened rats racing on a track I don't even know how I got onto in the first place. Was just moving to America enough?

My Saturn is afflicted in the second house of resources, money, and material wealth. That means that my relationship to money isn't rational. It's familial, anxious, dysphoric. It means that I know a lot about it, and I *still* don't get it. I know who in my peer group gets what their parents call "an allowance," and who has a trust; who paid for their own college, meaning they're in debt; who spends more than they earn; who earns more than they spend; who invests; who owns real estate; who's owed an inheritance; and who supports their own siblings or parents.

I know crypto-rich art bros, kids whose parents live next to the Clintons, Yale-sprung physicians, a middle-class, middle-American former cheerleader-cum-It-Girl, and a barely legal or-phaned dominatrix from Jersey who's hyped on class mobility. *Longevity, prosperity, give me the money*, she captions her 'grams. But I don't know, man. It's like, one minute I'm pissing in Lena Dunham's Hermès-orange luxury home bathroom, the next I'm looking at a man on the bus who only has one ear. He keeps trying to cover the open wound with his hand, only to have his arm get tired. He wears a straw bucket cap, his nails are tobacco stained like Lucien's, there's gauze caught in the wound, and I wish I could do something more than smile kindly and send healing energy when he looks my way, but this is just one abject reality of hundreds you'd see every day if you didn't actively ignore them like so many of us do.

My friend Peter suggested I'm actually obsessed with money—that that's my problem: "It's all you can see." A week after he said that, in the dark, after a long workday, I drove my roommate's car through this tight, curved archway with bright white pylons on the side of the lane. I was looking at them, to avoid hitting them, and so of course then I did. Peter's right. *You're supposed to look where you want to go.* My problem is that where I want to go—it's a long, unknown way from here.

When I couldn't make rent at twenty-six, twenty-seven, twenty-eight, it was like my veins were made of cold lead. I'd feel panic, stuck, dead—then I'd visualize slitting my wrists. The visual would just come, over and over again. I'd manically apply for jobs listed online that'd never call me back, create *another* new sugar baby profile, pace the blocks around my apartment, gather clothes to sell, and sell them for fourteen dollars. Blade to wrist to cold lead blood. Living hand-to-mouth and -landlord.

I first ended up at Mariposa because two to a room = my budget. But what I found there was realer than real estate. I've always been fascinated by connection: how you can meet someone who you'd think you'd get along with, who you might even admire, maybe you're even great pen pals—but when you get together in person, there's nothing there. And then there's the inverse. Why do some people stand out? When I interviewed Tilda Swinton, she called her friend-collaborators "my fellow travelers." Doesn't that feel true? Like you're passing through together? Within a few minutes of meeting Nadezhda, who is far more magnetic in person than online, where she tries too hard to get attention, I recognized her as one of my life's stars. *I wanna see her play.*

She can be an asshole but in a productive way. She's catalytic. Remember when I wrote that Nadezhda "studies machinery, systems, and code," and Morgan nutrition and fitness, and Alicia attachment and trauma? Nadezhda read that and wisely replied, "You know that's because that's what we each struggle with? I've always feared big systems. Since I was a little girl, I was terrified of bridges and the interiors of computers. Or my motorcycle, I had to learn how it worked"—she could fix it up herself, which I thought was so cool—"because it scared me. I wanted mastery over the unknown, over my fears."

Nadezhda noted that Morgan's knowledge of the body was bound to source-unknown addictions, while Alicia's emotional wisdom came from years of sociopolitical underprivilege, familial melodrama, and amorous relationship folly. Of course. What others experience as our gifts often come from our wounds. It's Simone, the artist of solace, who secretly yearns for the soothing, judgment-free company she gives so graciously to others. It's why I write, longingly, and can cook as elaborately—because rather than words of affirmation or touch, my parents nurtured through the mediums of books, meals, and cats. I remember when I told my friend Eric—then just a poet, now a social worker/poet—that my parents had never said "I love you," he replied, "Oh, of course you're a writer."

Words distract from my well-being, and yet I need them to counter the evil forces that keep us from well-being, like the lies of domination that organize our everyday, the myths of scarcity and competition. I wish I could stay quiet, but these pesky angels keep bullying me into advocacy. They tell me I have to tell you that in true equality, i.e., true diversity, i.e., our latent, gifted, given Reality, all competition is imaginary, as each individual is unique. How could we possibly compete?

After I canceled our reality show deal, I resolved to live 100 percent in the Real. I needed to practice *just being*, I thought, *so I'll stop being subtly coerced by malevolent forces.* Luckily, I was in LA, where I am happy to just be. Accepting a Franciscan vow of poverty, I walked the city for six months, talking to strangers and letting friends buy me coffee. I'd hang out with Rivington Starchild, who also didn't work. We'd sit for hours talking about our favorite authors, like Sun Ra and Aleister Crowley, who wrote, "Every man and every woman is a star." I wore clothes I found on the street and even canceled my phone plan, like Rivington and Lucien. I was inaccessible, like a boy, and more popular than ever. For someone who used to suffer from agoraphobic extremes of social anxiety, it stunned me how easy it was now to make friends. I'd never had a friend pick me up from an airport before then. I never thought someone I wasn't sleeping with would go so far out of their way for me.

I was living in what's still my all-time favorite bedroom. On Elden Avenue in Koreatown. I moved in after Miffany reclaimed her bed at La Mariposa. Inherited from Beau, Amalia's ex, my new room came furnished with a mattress, a low Japanese desk, bookshelves, lively plants, and a cartoon chili cheese dog—laminated art by Beau. Everything with a surface was yellow. A five-minute walk from Amalia's place, fifteen to Mariposa, my yellow room had an en suite bathroom, a balcony, and a mirrored wall. The balcony faced out onto the street, which was lined with those impossibly thin five-story palm trees, the kind that people move their cars out from under when the Santa Anas blow hard. I watched so many delicious characters arrive and leave from that balcony. Susan shimmied up the walkway to return a book I'd forgotten at her home. My new roommate, Dean (affable, funny, the best plus-one to any party), would bop out every afternoon, returning with sweet treats. Since I had no phone, Amalia would honk her Volvo's horn to let me know she was there for me. I'd wave down from my balcony like fucking Juliet. "Be right there!" I'd call out.

While Lucien was out of town for three blessed months, I dated Nadeem, the sweetest thing, a Cancer Sun skater who made his mom's favorite Afghan dishes for me. I saved my pocket change to take him, as thanks, to my favorite restaurant, a *cevichería* on Pico Boulevard run by a Guatemalan couple. The husband, Julio, was hosting and, mistaking Nadeem for Central American, he started joking with us about then Republican nominee and former reality TV star Donald Trump's promise to build a wall.

"What's a wall going to do?" Julio quipped. "Doesn't he know we're building an army? I go up and down Pico Boulevard every day. You know how many brown baptisms I see? Tens, hundreds. Mexican, Puerto Rican, Dominican. Go to a white church, how many babies are being christened? One a week, maybe? We'll be fine."

The less I expected from life, the richer my experience of it became. Wanting little, I recognized how much I'd always had. I came to understand—the only way you can, by living them— paradoxes that are so obnoxious when relayed to you as verbal counsel, like: *When you're grateful, you're given more. It's in letting go that you change the most.*

During this phase, to make the minimum I needed for rent, rice, greens, and beans, I returned to working as a celebrity journalist. This work, in years before, had pained me, because I was proud, and it was too close to what I really wanted to do: "write freely." Bound to systems of power and authority, I was bullied by editors into the kinds of ready-made forms and clichés that programmed me to be a phony, believing in the subliminal messaging of mass-market magazines as I had since I first started reading them at the age of ten: *Beauty is a skinny white girl. Money buys happiness. Freedom is the freedom to fashion oneself, to curate how you appear. Success is destiny, meritocracy. You can be whatever you want to be. Because you're worth it.* Bullshit.

It used to make me sick—how editors at top glossies only cared to cover what was "in," and how they were told what that was by the industries they serviced. Hollywood management, for instance, only allows "journalists" access to their "talent" when they have a "project" to promote. The talent is coached on what to say, and *what not* is in their contract. The easiest way to not fuck up is to say nothing of substance. Now I practiced not taking any of this personally, thanks to Dean, who also did this line of work. He said, "I just give my editors what they want: *The celebrity walked into the room ...*"

Before, I'd try to innovate form, spending hours writing far-out profiles and essays that'd inevitably get cut up in the name of style guides. Now I accepted the assignments as ways to survive and educate myself, a means to study success and corruption, and to practice my presence and humility. It was also an easy way to re-up on toilet paper. Most celebrity interviews take place in fancy hotels. I'd sit with a waning-in-fame pop star or an emerging It Girl for an hour, pick her brain, then I'd order a lavish lunch on the magazine's account, pretending it was for her, and before I left, I'd stuff my tote with shampoo, body lotion, rolls of toilet paper, and floral bouquets, and go back to where I finally felt at home.

That yellow room. I liked to sit on my yellow bed, on a milky crystal dildo, facing my wall of mirrors, meditating, with my eyes wide open behind closed lids. My spine would undulate without my trying. *Kundalini.* My being was orgasmic. I'd meditate on colors, or Lucien; sometimes I pictured hundreds of gender-free bodies jerking off with me. The best was when I could forget all earthly forms. I was just energy. It cycled through my body, radiating out, I'd contract to the infinite and back. Then I'd open my eyes and see how absurd I looked and laugh and laugh and laugh.

Once in that room, Lucien, back from one of his many trips, and very stoned, was riffing on Sun Ra and Arthur Russell. He'd YouTube DJ, layering songs and lectures, sometimes reading aloud to me. I had a hard time keeping up with his consumption. He was always either rolling or smoking a joint or cigarette, often both. This afternoon, Lucien tripped farther out than I'd seen him. He started moving around my room, trying on hats, jewelry, and sunglasses. In a particularly graceful ensemble—I think he was wearing plush tiger ears and a leather halter top—Lucien looked in my mirror and started talking to himself.

"Who's this guy?" He laughed, pointing at himself.

"Hello," he intoned. Then deeper: "*Hello*. Hell. Oh. Oh." He cracked up.

The room had gone sideways. Man was crazy as me! Lucien got it, the play of Maya, how illusive our avatars are. I'm always gawking at my reflection like, *Who the fuck is that?* That's the thing about vanity, it can actually be an embrace of the Great Mystery. It's so funny that we're in these skin suits, that I have a single thick hair I have to pluck from my chin every two weeks, that we walk around in clothes, as if we're not naked underneath, and that under that—I give blood to know I'm full of it, but doesn't it feel more like we're full of chasms and memories, of wind, charm, rhythms, weight, and divinity? And not only when we're on something. Sober reality—trust me—is the most psychedelic.

Episode 10—"Noogenesis"

"I'm going to write a book to save us," I told Morgan. "It's going to save all the girls and change the world."

Morgan was getting better, as I was getting worse—worse because I was judging my progress according to better or worse. I had had to move out of the yellow room, having accidentally given it to my friend Clara. It was a sublet situation, a miscommunication. While I had been in Mexico, Clara had assumed the room as hers, and she loved it. Clara loved living with Dean, just as he seemed to dig her, so when I returned, I figured it better that she stay—I'd go. A room had opened up in La Mariposa again, so I moved back in.

I was now 29.15, and that move, like almost everything I was doing, felt like a mistake. *I'm too old for this*, I thought. Nadezhda didn't do the dishes. There were cockroaches. Police choppers monitored the neighborhood. It was loud, and I was increasingly sensitive to sound. To everything. I wanted a baby. My body was getting all ready. This biological imperative, which had been creeping in since twenty-seven, when I first started lactating during ovulation, was now, thanks to Lucien, whose cum I fantasized about dousing my insides with, overwhelming my consciousness. *Thick cock tick tock thick cock tick tock this is the sound of your biological clock.* My PMS raged like, *Get seeded, you bitch!* My periods became mourning periods. I'd failed, again. *You can't have a baby,* reason taunted me. *You're broke with no prospects of Ever Making Money.*

Morgan, who was known to bike fifty miles to escape herself and who counted calories down to dried seaweed, had taken up yoga. "It's training my mind," she said, in awe of the practice. A new kind of discipline, new neural pathways, or whatever—it was working. Morgan said she felt more in control, and more important, more comfortable with not being.

Meanwhile, I was back to self-bullying.

Committing to the Real, I'd committed to the unknown, accepting my lowly station. But now I wanted something, and desire is dangerous. It'll keep you from the Real. I didn't just want, I *needed*, I thought, and stat: an adult means to money, a healthy home, and a baby, with Lucien. Poor kid.

29.15, 29.25, 29.33: I kept thinking, *I wanna die.* Then Clara would write to say, "That's 'cause a part of you is!" We exchanged texts like:

Wild how humans still judge what we don't understand
Wild how a fingernail can cover the sun!!

"I forgot the cosmic joke!" was my gag line at the time.

I was taking everything *so seriously*. Mainly my lack of money. Whereas in younger years I was convinced everything that was wrong with my life had to do with my not being pretty, thin, or fun enough, now my obsessional lack was money. It's the same: The psychology of scarcity. Confusing your being with being of popular social value. As a young, girl-identified thing, your pop value is suppleness, nubility, *maybe* precocity, though clever is the smartest you should be. There was a time when I wanted to be a girl in a magazine. Airbrushed, contained. I know I'm not alone in having wanted this because the latest real-life beauty trend is HD pore-free perfection. Contouring the face and bust as image, cast in shadow and light. And preventative Botox: "Do you want a static look?" they ask. I wanted to be so beautiful, I wouldn't have to do anything but be beautiful. I wanted to just be. Pouty, languid. Touch me! Immediacy. Hot and cool and empty. Contemporary advertising is so insidious because it conflates genuine human drives (emptiness is grace) with an image and a product promising to deliver such inspired states of being.

Money money money money!

Someone once told me the reason songs get stuck in our head is because the mind wants to hear them to completion. Remembering only a refrain, it'll repeat. The best way, then, to get a song out of your head is to listen to the whole thing.

But no one would talk with me about money. *The last taboo.* I'd try bringing it up, this thing I was genuinely struggling with, and people would default to platitudes or change the topic.

It's possible that no one wanted to talk about money because they could tell how hot a topic it was for me. I was easily spun into spells of anxiety. They didn't want to be responsible for that; I wasn't response-able. Or maybe God, the Universe, or I, or whatever wanted me to figure it out for myself. UGHRRGH!

In the midst of this, I started noticing my Kundalini instructor, Guru Mitar, repeat: "We can't overcome real problems head-on. We have to go about them sideways. That's why we lift our arms up to sixty degrees."

Movies have made my consciousness impatient for change. I expect challenging transformations to occur over the course of one song as a montage. Not jumping into freeway traffic cut tearful praying at a bus stop cut leaving the library with teetering stacks of books cut underlining passages like a maniac cut looking like I had an epiphany cut dancing in my bedroom *fade* dancing in the club cut laughing with friends over cocktails cut cutting my own hair cut looking amazing with my new haircut at a business meeting cut shaking hands cut bank balance over a hundred— no—over *a thousand* dollars cut buying myself flowers, driving a convertible into the sunset, cut cut cut.

Ha ha ha. A vortex of change did hit me, actually. But it was nothing like that.

Ariana, a poet, artist, and astrologer whose work I revered, had told me this was coming. During a natal chart reading the month I moved back into Mariposa, she said, "Between January and May, you won't feel like yourself." I'd forgotten she told me this until February, when—depressed and desperate for counsel—I decided to re-listen to the audio recording of her reading. There it was, her prediction: "Barren, confusing, you won't be able to delight in others as usual. Perhaps a time of more reading and writing."

I told Nadezhda it felt like a spiritual puberty. Like changes were happening that were beyond my control; mysterious, awkward, uncertain. Nadezhda had been spritely lately—twenty-two, in love, and adventuring. This kept me going. Everything is always happening at once: birth, death, love, loss. If I could just focus on this—the all—I wouldn't self-destruct in my individualized WTF. The thing was, most people in my world were suffering. Simone was exhausted, working overtime in the slog of cold-winter Canada. Misty was uncharacteristically anxious on a residency in Athens. Alicia was burned out on bad flames in Brooklyn. And Lucien kept threatening suicide on the phone from Taos. Trump had just taken office. They say your Zen practice only really starts when the going gets rough. It's easy to be breezy when love's abundant—in that yellow room, meditating on bliss.

"Sometimes I wonder," Alicia once mused, "if this realm isn't a forced labor camp for the expansion of universal consciousness, like if our working through suffering isn't somehow energy building. We're God's slaves."

Another theory of the Universe we shared is that we're transitioning into the Age of Aquarius. We figured ourselves as early Aquarian heroines, tasked with bringing about the New Age and its promised dissolution of imperialist Western supremacist capitalist patriarchy. We're in the midst of a paradigm shift. Gender flux, collective consciousness, interconnectivity, respect—this is all dawning, but just. We may not see the clearing in our lifetime. Next time I'm coming back as a cat, or a tree. Human beings are exhausting.

I missed Alicia. It seemed like everyone was always coming and going and coming and going. The twenty-first-century way. We moved through cities, gigs, and trends like we flipped channels as kids. I knew I had friends all over the world—I watched them online—but none were here for me now, or I couldn't be Real around those who were, "Because I'm an alien!!" (My version of Morgan's aquarium.)

My alienation was unlike anything I'd experienced before. I knew unruly states. I used to get so furious with desire, I'd want to set fire to Pasadena family homes, put cigarettes out on my forearms, smash in windshields, and bind my throat in stems of thorns. I knew envy's venom, and the spiky thrill of cynical intellection conquering disappointment, and I knew the hollowness that followed. I knew demoralization, and self-pity, and anxiety. But this? This was a feeling like antigravity, but with no emotional levity. My mind felt like a bowl of jelly that had been slurped by some unknown force until all that was left were a few quivering scraps in my skull. Even the baby idea, my umbilical cord to the world, had started to seem ridiculous.

This is the part of the book where readers complain I've lost them.

"The narrator disappears," they say. "My attention waned . . . I couldn't connect to anything."

Amen.

This was a part of my life when, if you were to figure it cinematically, you'd set everything including the soundtrack to slooow-moootioon and add some gooey g1itC#hy% FULL-SCREEN distortion.

I called it being an alien, because I had no human reference for what was happening. I tried describing my new phenomenology to friends, but when I did, they looked in my direction as if I wasn't there, just as I blanked out whenever they started talking about restaurants, movies, or a package they had lost in the mail, you know, "the real world"—it was utterly unrelatable.

I walked LA now nauseated by its smells, like piss, fast food, and gasoline. I watched office buildings bend on the face of other office buildings, reflections in windows wavering as I walked by over and over again, transfixed by the curves. I walked into twelve guns, police pistols pointed at a black man on 8th in Koreatown. I took my phone out to film it. Most citizens walked right on by. Everyday life in our crumbling empire—maybe my dad was right.

The latest trends in the high fashion I followed were clowns and cowboys. Whiteface makeup on models in high-end designs mirroring the grotesquerie of white supremacy, its renewed visibility in our political climate. On a similar tip, Alicia said she was suddenly drawn, and she wasn't the only one, to Wild West styles—the hats, boots, and chaps in dusty leathers and suede: "As a way to assert my Americanness at the same time it's being denied."

"The flag"—I overheard a homeless person scream—"looks like sheriff badges and blood!"

It was windy season in Los Angeles, so the national flags, which usually hung just out of my short-statured, self-involved line of sight, were suddenly thwapping louder than choppers, unignorable and everywhere, I realized.

A man was murdered in our building. His lover, a young woman, who I'd met for the first time in our lobby that very morning (she looked like Beyoncé and had a baby; we talked about worn T-shirts and my mom) had stabbed him. Self-defense. I tried following up on her case through neighbors, police, journalists, and our landlord. No word.

Life was all dead ends and detours: nausea, stasis, sleep. It had to be some kind of puberty because I was angst-ridden with shame about my new reality, and sleeping nine, ten, twelve hours a night, as if I was growing. My waking hours were occupied by books, including this one. It was then: cornered in the east wing of La Mariposa, only enough money saved for rent, and jobless—no assignments, all my pitches and applications denied—that I started writing for myself again. Episode 02—in which we meet Noo.

One of the purposes of our Saturn Returns, I read, is to empower us to become authors of our own lives. *Reclaiming your authority*, I read on a blog, *means taking responsibility for whatever is happening in your life.*

I used to give so much of myself away. In my teens and early twenties, in the name of experimentation, I flowed. I tried on belief systems and friends like I did clothes. Near the end of my third decade, this started to feel scary. Like repercussions were real, consequences could be lasting. My mind started sorting inventories of everything I'd done and how it'd played out; where I'd fucked up, been cruel or neglectful, what I'd loved and lost. It seemed suddenly like I'd mistaken *bending to others' wills* with *going with the flow*, like I'd been all too organized by my parents, schools, media, peers, and history.

Is this who I want to be? What is an "I"?

For years, I've been studying the violence inflicted through language. Bullying, insults, property contracts, religious dogma, binary opposition, and propaganda. When I first met La Mariposa, convinced our alphabet wrought more evil than good, I started fantasizing about a *Tower of Babel: The Sequel.*

In this twenty-first-century version of the story, humankind—who are going mad talking and typing, telling and [unintelligibly yelling]—would be struck mute. All of us! We'd all get severe aphasia. We'd still be able to hear: breath, moans, sighs, the sounds of words and surrounding nature, but their signification would be lost to us. Or their denotation? Yeah, that, because we'll still be able to hear pitch, tone, and the musicality and feeling of speech. We won't be able to read either. We'll see letters and words as nothing but shapes!

Now if this were to happen, what I believe we'd learn is that some of us are subtly psychic. Or, said another way, there are many ways to communicate, and some of us are more attuned to those than others. Body language, intuition, empathy. We who are lit like that would become superheroes. Persecuted, probably, like the X-Men. Or like we already are.

"The goal is to invent a language without othering," says my friend Jac, a trans woman who's been diagnosed as schizophrenic and so can't get legit gender-reassignment help. She has a hard time getting by, making rent or non-Internet friends, and this is why I don't get our world—I think she's right about almost everything, and yet she's so afraid she can barely leave her state-assisted bare-bones housing.

I didn't trust my use of language—that's why I quit writing for a spell. I realized I'd been using it to get things, like attention. I relied on ready-made linguistic transactions to survive. I wrote press for a living, and I always regretted it: hackneyed phrasing, stereotyping. Nothing hurts me more than saying what I don't mean or saying mean things. I've been beaten up, bones broken, covered in tattoos, but none of that hurt compares with the pain of betraying the truth we all hold, the better we know to do. This is why I quit writing, but that's a lie! I'm always writing. I can't stop. This fucking mind. I quit *publishing* because language organizes lives, and my language, I realized, was corrupt and corrupting. I'd learned it from mass media, duh, from commerce. Lies lies lies.

I'm serious about saving us. Every time I say it, I get goose bumps. It's like my third-favorite astrologer Kelley Rosano insists: *We don't get what we need, we get what we believe.*

I've started to believe that writing is magic. Check it: s-p-e-l-l-s.

William S. Burroughs, one of my philosophical heroes, who

occasionally communicated misogyny and who lived on an allowance from Mommy into his fifties, is often quoted as having said: *Language is a virus from outer space.* I think because it's mysterious. It infects us. Has side effects. Evil thoughts and utterances will manifest in physical dis-ease and other gnarly realities. Ditto banality. And godliness.

When I moved to LA, I'd just started to consciously try to wield what Burroughs called "the Wishing Machine." This is the idea that there's some sort of universal mechanism wherein what we ask for will be delivered, but of course its timing and totality may be unexpected. *Be careful what you wish for.*

I've manifested boyfriends. Before the comic book boy, I said, "I need to learn about health and nutrition," and there he was: a young man with a chronic illness he managed via holistic means. Before Lucien: "I want to learn about the esoteric arts, magic, spirit, and acting. I want to act." Welcome: my devious actor lover, a prince of darkness, and Jesus freak. (I used to use boyfriends as a secondary education. It's like my friend Misty once said, "Ever notice how men have so much ... information?")

When I told Morgan I would write a book to save myself and her and all the girls, I believed it, because I'm desperate. I never want to play dead again. I never want to disappear so far into myself that people I've known for years cease to recognize me in person. (This happened in my anxious New York years, and when my old friends finally understood—"Oh, you're *Fiona, Fiona*"—it was with a look of horror I'll never forget.) I mean it because I need you. I need my fellow travelers, co-conspirators, playmates, wizards. But seriously! Who else will I hang out with in heaven? There are heavens on Earth. Don't kill yourself yet, Simone! Don't drown in self-hate, Morgan! It's inevitable, we'll die eventually, so until then, can we please have some fun? I know it's tempting to go in, to fall out of the Real—fear is ready-made, *marketed to us*—I fall for it too, but when you do: I miss you.

Amalia lately is distracted, frustrated, and tired, cursing the art world, which is disinterested in her latest, most novel work, which in a decade, when it's less politically relevant, you know they'll be mad for. Meanwhile Simone, savior mother sweet, keeps sending me pictures of the rashes that are exploding all over her body, as her beloved *nonna* is dying, her career is sputtering before starting, and she's being kicked out of another apartment building (this one's been bought out by a bro-y tech start-up). I can't get through to Mo. Or, we talk, and I know she's hearing me, registering it all, but her fear is louder, and fucking with her. I have a sense this fear was ignited by the house fire and the boyfriend she got with thereafter who was into gagging blow jobs. His kink was making the girl puke, which Mo did once (she's always been good-giving-game), and she said she felt disgusting after ("humiliated, ashamed"). Worse still, this boy, who should've been a man (he's thirty-four), confessed he was still in love with his ex-girlfriend *the whole year* he and Mo were dating. Stop wasting our time!

I know the Wishing Machine is Real because I've started paying attention. As my articulated desires become clearer and more heartfelt, they manifest faster and more obviously, with less corrupt by-products. When I broke the reality show contract, my practice was still clumsy.

I remember walking around Ktown one evening, probably PMSing, feeling out of sorts, furious and in mourning. Pulse, the gay nightclub in Orlando, Florida, had just been shot up by a man in the midst of his Saturn Return. When I saw the picture of the perpetrator, Omar Mateen, a twenty-nine-year-old security guard, I said: "He's gay." I just knew. Eventually, it was reported that various witnesses recognized Mateen from Pulse and gay dating apps. The FBI claimed that wasn't what was up, and blamed the motive on "terrorism," the Islamic State. But self-denial, feeling Other and apart, ashamed, confused, and repressed in your desires—I don't know anything more motivating to violence.

I, too, have wanted to hurt what I most desired, that which I was and wasn't. I hated my high school crush Ashley Anne Cooper. I hated luscious girly girls who could just! have! fun! I hated the boys I loved because I wanted to be loved like them. I wanted to destroy everything I wanted to be or be with but felt I couldn't or wasn't allowed.

On this heated evening in Ktown, I was on my fucking phone again, talking into its Voice Memos app:

the psychology that leads to such fantastic violence,
the reality bleed,
impotence, disbelief, screen-addled everything and nothing,
the vigor of destruction
it's easier to destroy than to create,

destruction is seductive, and
—lazy, common, fear based—
it's scary to try and actually make a difference
to change
Just then, I saw a group of girls in a car. Young women playing loud music, filling up their gas tank. I melted—
That's never been me.
I want that.
I want to just be with girlfriends,
to go on an adventure,
in a car.
I was precise. I cried.

(I barely cried for a decade. My phony years. Stuck up. Now
I cry daily. "Me too," Clara says. "I think of it like sweating. You
gotta do it all the time. Let the toxins out.")

The next week, I found myself at Manhattan Beach with
Alicia, Clara, and Nadezhda. Clara and I had taken a touch of
acid, drinking it from a shared glass of water in that yellow room,
and then we piled into Alicia's car to drive to the beach. As soon
as we parked, Clara leaned out of her passenger-side door and
pissed onto hot concrete. I almost peed my pants laughing.

At the beach, we cuddled on a blanket and waded into the
ocean. Clara delighted in the water; she looks so much like
Laura Dern when she smiles. The acid was mild, all it added
was some rainbow brights to the sea-foam. A group of dudes
tried making lame moves on Alicia. She says this happens everywhere she goes, that it's incessant and physical. "Sometimes
men think they can pick me the fuck up." She's like one hundred

pounds, five foot two? Alicia was discomfited by the attention. We gossiped until the sun clouded over, then packed up, and drove the long way home, singing along ("I love this song!") with Rihanna and Lil Wayne.

We had to stop for gas along the way. As I watched petite Alicia pumping fuel into her car, I, too, got filled up with what I privately call God. A warmth of stillness in gratitude. When you recognize your wishes fulfilled, don't forget to say thank you.

Episode 11—"All the Real girls"

IF YOU'RE IN AN ABUSIVE relationship, it's likely you believe people can change. Or you're intimate with their pain. It's textured like yours, or like your little brother's, who you wished you could heal but never could. Sex is a salve you can deliver now. Or maybe you grew up starved for attention, so this possessiveness feels like what you missed.

Maybe you love seeing what will happen next. Being with them was like playing roulette at first. You'd either get nothing or a prize, but then triggers were introduced, and now it's more like Russian roulette: same game of chance, higher stakes.

You're accustomed to being on high alert. To living in a home wherein one wrong spill or sentence could incite a fight. And you love them. And you want to believe. *I love you I love you I love you*, they say, dragging you by the feet. You're ashamed for wanting to believe, you should know better. Or maybe you're scared of your own rage, so you use theirs to access it. What do you know? You've never been alone long enough to hear your interior.

They are your only mirror. You have no friends, no family, no money—or you think you don't—and you can't make it without them. You've been bullied into insecurity. Or you're proud, so you believe: *You can't hurt me.* And you're definitely raunchy, horny, a devious slut, and no one else lets this vital side of you out.

Or maybe you're a writer. A method writer, an everyday life actress, dangerously curious and curiously dangerous. An evil succubus stealing their life story because you're not creative enough to invent your own.

In high school in Ottawa, Ontario, I remember the boys used to have us line up according to height, twelve girls in a row, so they could slap our asses in a crescendo. Once, we volunteered to line up according to bra size. Not yet knowing I had perfect, puffy-nipped Lolita tits, I was humiliated to be first in line. In the nineties and early aughts, where I grew up, prime girldom— womanhood—was all about big titties. I knew the bra size of every one of my friends, just as I knew their grade point average. We competed in every domain in which we were rewarded: looks, grades, popularity.

I remember, once, we made this known. At Sybil's house, one afternoon after school, our clique confessed to our miscellaneous rivalries: how I was jealous, but actually awed, by Ash's effortless holistic perfectionism; how Dawn's 98 percent made us feel dumb; how we wished Sybil's photogenic nuclear family was our own; and how we each felt too ugly, thin, fat, or flat. Six fifteen-year-old white girls hysterically crying, exchanging judgments as compliments, and compliments as judgments. We all hugged at the end, went home, and never talked about it again.

Remember when I told you I went to Oaxaca City on an art residency? That's where I was when Saturn hit the exact degree it was in relation to Earth when my already hairy head screamed for the first time. I was marked with a Scorpio Rising, just like Lucien. They say that relates to a difficult birth. My mom will say she's "not so sure" about that; that she, like me, "has a pelvic construction perfect for popping them out—it was easy."

"No," I'll reply, knowing this isn't entirely true. "I know I didn't want to be born in London, Ontario. I'm a Californian baby, and you took that away from me."

I remember the first time I saw Lucien. It was at Café Gratitude on Rose Avenue in Venice Beach, and he was all thin and tweaky, styled like a hippie and acting as if he'd time traveled from when our parents were young, reckless, and wild. Since a friend had told me about him, I knew something Lucien didn't yet: that he was raised in the house I'd gazed at pictures of my whole life. My almost life: it'd been alive inside me for twenty-seven years, and now it was standing in front of me, clearly wasted, longing, on edge. I prayed Lucien wasn't a junkie, because I knew I'd follow him anywhere.

Right before I met Lucien, I had made two resolutions. One, I would no longer date entitled pretty boys. Two, I would practice aligning my intentions, communications, and actions, meaning I would mean what I say and say what I mean, and behave accordingly. The mystery of life makes this tricky. As soon as Lucien showed up, I knew I'd break both resolutions.

For over two years, he lived inside me. The music we listened to together played on repeat. Every orgasm came with a sound of him. Our studies intermingled—Krishnamurti, Stanislavsky, Reality. Lucien and his friends could afford to live in the Real, it seemed, unlike me and mine. They tripped beyond the confines of their minds and screens, to Paris, Taos, Tokyo, and Desert Hot Springs. They played real instruments, like grand pianos and violins, and lived in real big apartments they could afford without having to pretend to be something they weren't. My girlfriends and I strived to get what they had: enough time and space to create. Washing hair, babysitting, waitressing, and sugar babying, we faked pleasantries, dissociated, to get it done and go. But everything you do becomes you. My internal tempo from thirteen to twenty-seven was go go go. If I just do this, then maybe I'll get that. It was promised. *You can be anything.* I took it too literally. I tried to shape-shift, work hard, people please, act.

When I met Lucien, I'd already started to let go of all notions of self and other bad habits I'd taken on in order to "make it." I was open. And then we met, and this still feels Real, whenever I think of him: I know myself. I'm no name—I never identified with my name. I'm not this body—it keeps changing. I'm not my parents—what a chance occurrence. I'm a resonance, a texture, a chord. The heartstrings are no metaphor!

Lucien had been supposed to join me in Oaxaca. Instead, I got a story. A young woman named Miranda showed up at my apartment gate on Elden Avenue to meet Clara, who had been subletting my blessed yellow room while I was away. Miranda had driven seven hours from the Bay to meet a boy she'd had a romance with in Austin, Texas, a few months before. His name was Lucien Langham and when she arrived in Los Angeles, after he had been the one to encourage her to come, he didn't return any of her texts or calls, just like he'd done to me before. Meanwhile, Lucien had been talking to me.

I was researching flights to Mexico for Lucien when Miranda called Clara, a girl she knew online, looking for a place to crash. What a beautiful coincidence. Miranda and I had the exact same Fuchs brand red recycled-plastic toothbrush. Same apple cheeks. Clara sent me a picture of Miranda in my bathroom, our two toothbrushes lined up next to each other.

Miranda and Clara ended up having an affair. For two nights, they hooked up in the very bed—on my one set of sheets—that Lucien and I had unmade so many times before. When Clara texted to tell me, I was hit with envy: Clara was always hooking up with girls besides me!

When I first met Clara, I had thought I wanted her, but then I did what I default to with girls: I made her a sister. Within fifteen minutes of meeting, Clara was undressing in front of me. She had to try on this Prada Sport ensemble a professional woman we both admired had just gifted her. A miniskirt and halter top. Clara has the type of body people want to dress and undress. She was manic that first meeting. It didn't seem ethical to seduce her, I thought, like I, too, would be taking advantage of her.

Over the next couple of years, Clara and I got close, close enough to call each other sister, and that's how I learned, through her casual telling, how often she ended up fucking when she "wasn't so into it." Subtly coerced into a threesome; raped by a sugar daddy who she did have a boner for before, but not in the way he ended up in her. Clara seemed open to advances, I guess. Pliable. She submitted easily to performative authority and "believed the best in people." This often meant ignoring their bad behavior, or justifying it like: *Well, what they really mean to share is love, I can feel it, but they're wounded so …* Even though she's tall, strong, naturally athletic, and creepy smart, Clara consistently lets iffy people direct her life experiences for their own sexual benefit, to her detriment, and this question haunted me: Why?

When Lucien was in Austin with Miranda, he had been writing of his *undying love* for me. I forgave him again and again. I forgave him when a barely legal–looking girl came up to me to tell me she was a fan of my writing, and then when she saw who I was texting, said, "That guy has been messaging me too, like explicitly." I forgave him when he threatened "to O.J." any new lover I took, and when he cried suicide every time I said I was leaving him, a clear manipulation. I even forgave him after a blond model entered my Sex and Love Addiction recovery group and started detailing a boy she was dating who sounded *just like Lucien.* He was the one who had suggested I enter the program—because I refused to commit to him—and I, being open to experience, or something, agreed to try it. The program had me cut ties with Lucien. *You're not supposed to engage with your addictions while recovering.* Then this young woman came in, well into a relationship with him, longer into it than I'd been in the program. It was him, I later confirmed via three verifiable sources. I'm a journalist, kid! It's like he wanted to get caught.

In Mexico, I'd found him flights like he'd asked, and even arranged a chaste sugar baby date to help pay for our life when he arrived. The date went as so many of my sugar-baby dates did—we'd talk about politics and familial psychodynamics and then I'd get a kiss on the cheek and an envelope of cash at the end.

Eduardo was Spanish and Mexican. He ran his family's dairy farm. He'd never been married or even close. He was forty-five, and he told me that at forty he had suffered a severe depression.

"In Mexico, we don't have mental illness," he said, meaning it's not socially recognized.

I remember seeing a hand-painted sign for NEURÓTICOS ANÓNIMOS by a highway in Oaxaca City. An anime-style boy in a hoodie and jeans held his hands to his face in anguish. *Neurotics Anonymous.*

"Here," Eduardo explained, "life is pain. You're supposed to endure, keep quiet, find God."

Eduardo believed in the same kind of God as me: "There's something—serendipity, mystery, *all this* . . ." We drank a fulsome Spanish red at the most expensive restaurant in Oaxaca City and talked about the local teachers' strike, American colonialism and military intervention, and the "harmony ideology" practiced between indigenous Oaxacan populations.

While in Mexico, I had been dropped by a publisher for writing "too subjectively" and "unbelievably." "Problematic." They were right, and not. I was writing from inside madness. It wasn't unreal—in fact, many femmes found it relatable—but my book was definitely not set in the Real. It was sick, sad, and yearning—like I was about to get in the extreme: I caught a parasite or two. Convinced I could fight it off alone, because I didn't want to pay for a doctor, I hid in my room suffering for a week until it was clear this was fucking stupid.

I had gotten sick the day I realized Lucien wasn't coming.

Lucien Langham got $3K from his trust every month, and he wouldn't even split the cost of my morning-after pill when he was the one who got too excited months into our relationship. "It's your body," he said. "I wouldn't want to interfere." He always left my place with a keepsake: a lighter, a ball cap, sunglasses, parking passes, books. I'd never see these things again. Things were always being "stolen" from him. When we first started hanging out, he requested "a simple favor": that I not tell mutual friends we were involved. "I'm famous, Fiona," he said. "People love to talk." Then he'd share excessive poetic visions of marrying me, tell me I'm so smart, have me promise to be "a good girl," meaning faithful. He said he would "always be here" for me, then be unreachable for weeks. And somehow, he had a psychic radar for whenever I was moving on. Every time I started going out with new people, as dates or just as friends, Lucien would show up again, often on my doorstep, late at night, pacing and cursing me out. Once he punched his car, breaking skin. Another time, he smashed a glass bottle at my feet. "Liar!" he screamed, when I insisted I hadn't been with anyone but him. "Even thinking about it is a betrayal," he said. I clocked all these red flags as they waved in my face, but why did I stay for so long?

I loved the dirt behind his fingernails, the slant of his brown eyes, and his smell, like cigarettes, sweat, and the lingering musk from boy-branded grooming products. Lucien smelled like a boy! I loved how he taught me to wake up with no idea of what to do, and how he reminded me to walk slow and take back alleys. I loved all the music he played: Croatian synth pop, Bobby Caldwell slowed and chopped, Blaze Foley, Kendrick Lamar, Fleetwood Mac's *Tusk*, and Jackie DeShannon singing about what the world needs now. I loved the music from his iPhone crackling out on my Bluetooth speaker as he left my home, like the way he'd let his cigarettes burn out, distracted by his own talktalktalk.

On the radio, I once overheard Camille Paglia say offhand that what we don't talk about when we talk about abusive relationships is how the sex is so good. Paglia insisted that's why so many women stay in them. They call us victims, say it's about our subjugation, cite Stockholm syndrome. Yes, but there's the animal. Women are wild too. The sex wasn't even *that* good. Lucien could be lazy, he came all too fast, and didn't luxuriate in oral (I need you to genuinely *love it* for me to surrender on your mouth). But the energy. Fucking cosmic or biological destiny, I wanted his seed in me. The heart between my legs beat cartoonish for him. Sticky thighs and selfies. I learned how beautiful I was around him. I loved making out in cars, alleys, and on the beach. Lucien kissed like a girl. He must have kissed hundreds of girls. I kept telling him, *We don't need to be monogamous, I know you're not, do what you want, just don't lie to me.*

But he did, and even though I knew, I repeated: "I love you." I told others too: "I love him," "He's a piece of shit," "A li'l liar with tiny—" "But God, I love that kid."

And I believed it. Totally, fully, full of it.

I love him, I thought, because every time I meditated on him, my psyche cleared, my heart lifted, the Real came into focus, and I knew myself. Our love felt incorruptible. Man could kill me, and I'd still love him. It was *Krazy Kat* shit. We were both Krazy and Ignatz. I loved torturing him and getting slapped.

Maybe the feeling isn't love, I wrote in my diary in the swollen dumb heart of it. *Maybe it's power? I don't know. Language can only paw at the door of sensation.*

And create it. Looking back, I see how Lucien Langham cast spells on me. You know, s-p-e-l-l-s. He told me all these things I wanted to hear. Stories of Ancient Egypt, Native America, Old Hollywood, and Point Dume back in the day. He told me: *People will listen to you, Fiona. You could be a really important writer.*

Love is the answer. No one feels better. We need you for the revolution. I prefer bush. I don't know if he meant any of it, or if he's just that skilled a manipulator, discerning what his target wants to hear. And I don't really care because I'm so grateful to have learned what it is I want to hear.

After Oaxaca, when I ghosted to the Bay to cat-sit Albert and Nabokov, my life was like this: I'd follow any gig or trade that would allow me the time and space I needed to create. Instead of writing for publications, I painted, meditated, read, and wrote and wrote and wrote copious dumb notes about what was wrong with me, my family history, society, the economy, God help me. During one meditation, seated on the carpeted floor of this beautiful home that belonged to one of my mom's friends (they were closest right before I was born), I gave birth to myself. I was two days back from Oaxaca, and this was painful, ecstatic, and the most fearsomely calm I've ever felt.

I realized I had died in Mexico. My rose-lensed romanticism had died. My unreality had died. I had gotten sick, I was taken care of, and I died. Lucien never came. The publisher dropped me. I ran out of money. In a tiny clay room, puking and shitting, sweating and sleeping, I had prayed for all the women in my life to come take care of me. Visions of Alicia wiping my brow, Simone serving me broth, Amalia cracking jokes, and my mother whispering good night. When I was a girl, I used to love getting sick, because it was one of the only times I was guaranteed my ambitious mom's attention. She'd tuck me in and check back in throughout the night, and in the morning, taking my temperature, her hands couldn't avoid touching my cheek.

I sat cross-legged and so open-hipped my pubis touched the floor. I meditated into this split consciousness. I was simultaneously pure sensation and observing without judgment. The sensation was an undulation from my pelvic floor up to my spine and out the top of my head. I was rocking without willing it. "I" wasn't doing anything as I passed through black to pink and red and back: excruciating pain; a damp, wet, raw opening; pleasure and pain. An orgasm, a deep, earthy, gross orgasm that decomposed as it rose, durational and shuddering, chaotic and quiet.

Eclipsing the light, the visionary sensations ended with my floating in space, in this lonely, cold place, which I'd caught a glimpse of in the desert with David. Now I sat in it for a long time. I felt convinced I'd just experienced being born and giving birth, where we come from, and where we return. I felt my mother very close. I understood her wary wisdom, and why we fear women, because this place isn't heavenly, easy, or light. It's bitter, dark, fresh like humus, and Real, collective, suspenseful, antigravitational. Beautiful.

The Real is a reminder of death. It's the eternal now. It's Maya, discerning illusion and sensing deeper. It's taking responsibility, it's being in the flow. It's heavy, funny, and light. Fluid, paradoxical, holy shit. And it can be painful. Humiliating. Some people live here—where actions have consequences, where magic is enacted. Here, you have agency and guidance. Your heart is your compass. *You feel what's right and true.* It may be ineffable, but it's not ephemeral—the Real is the most material state I know.

The Real can be painful. When did we learn to escape? Was I a kid bored in class? Was it when that man descended on me, if he did? Was it when I realized that the collective imaginary, the "real world" imaginary, like Disney and Wall Street, was in direct conflict with my interior life? The imagination is Real. I can look at your face and picture it melting, and it does. The thing about imaginary things is they disappear as fast as you envision them. They're as unreliable as words unless you make them matter. Materialize them.

Being with Lucien was like smoking. An image and fantasy I craved. Delight on the lips. A practiced suck that made me smolder. Late at night it felt so good. The next day, though, I'd be queasy, edgy, and craving more more more. In the short term, my indulgence would be coupled with other bad habits. I'd start drinking: fire for fire. Then need: weight to absorb the hurt. Bacon breakfast burritos with black coffee, another smoke. I'd get lazy, stop meditating. And think: cynically. Obsessing over elusive desire, I'd fail to show up for friends and family, ignore work opportunities. My life, every time I let him back in, would devolve—plain bad luck punctuated the mundane. Then I'd cut him out and repair myself, and fortune would find me again. But I couldn't resist testing this. Friends called me a masochist.

Like smoking, the glamour of self-ruin I delighted in was fun for a while, but in the long term I knew its accumulated reality could kill me.

Another analogy for my relationship to Lucien came directly from him. A few months into his sobriety, he was spouting program gospel endlessly. We were driving through the Santa Monica mall one afternoon when he said, "Alcoholism is a simultaneous obsession with, and allergy to, alcohol." I turned to him and said, "But love! That's how I feel about you."

Unbeknownst to me, during my last phase of devotion to Lucien, three girlfriends of mine, Clara, Misty, and Alicia, smart girls, were each mired in their own abusive dynamic with a volatile young man. That's a mark of relationships like these: we hide them from loved ones. I learned of Clara's idiot when, months into the romance, she shared screencaps of his messages to her, which had finally escalated, she realized, beyond something she could keep private. He called her a bitch, a whore, and more, threatened violence, samo samo. Alicia's and Misty's guys stalked them after my friends tried to break up with them. I'd be hanging with Alicia or Misty, and see an ex lurking down the street, waiting for me to leave, so they could catch their prey alone.

The guys knew to cry when they apologized. "I'm sorry, I fucked up." He didn't mean to punch Misty. He didn't mean to destroy Alicia's art portfolio. He didn't mean those things he said to Clara. These guys were vulnerable when it served them, lavishly expressing their woundedness—"I didn't mean to"—which we lapped up, because we hurt too, but less, so much less, when we were helping them.

"It's a movie," Alicia told me. "The one-to-one intensity. You can get caught up. Especially if, you know, when you're in it, you're getting dick four times a day. It's also probably something like mistaking adrenaline from fear for passion, and longing for love."

Freedom is what I was after. That feeling of nothing constricting your chest, of mobility, bouncy ease. But like longing can be confused for love, and fear for passion, freedom can be mistaken for *reaction*: fleeing, fighting, feeling what you need to be *free from*.

The Boys. It's their confidence I wanted. *Their entitlement.* Seemingly uncaring of what others thought, and lauded for it. Cowboys. Skater boys. With evasive gazes and unadulterated eyelashes, long, thick, and naked. The groove of their chests. Their turning their backs. Shrugs and hair flips and poor grades: a demonstration of their intelligence, being above normative structures. Casualness in business rewarded with big money. Their freedom. Their autonomy. My fantasy.

Lucien wasn't the first, he was just the ultimate Boy. Me if I were one. We have the same curve of ass. The same sensitive skin that breaks out on our back. The same professed values and taste in justice and art. And the way we looked at girls as these mystical creatures that got our dicks hard and in so doing momentarily solved it all: our self-loathing, our resenting the real world for making us feel like pieces of shit, our acting like pieces of shit.

My friends Chloe and Flan (they're in a band, with the best lyrics, called Odwalla 1221) named the archetype: "Butterflies." Chloe laughed when she said it. "Carefree popular pseudo-free spirit boys." Yes. Butterflies in my stomach, butterfly kisses on my pussy lips, social butterflies, elusive, pretty, flying flowers, he loves me, he loves me not.

What I wanted from Lucien, more than being with him, was to be him. Narrow-hipped, a dick. Moneyed, cultured, an artist. Articulate. The mean things he said to me were just more eloquent versions of what I'd been telling myself daily since puberty. *You're dumb, fake, fat, inexperienced, ignorant, and too smart for your own good.*

A false concept of mind versus heart was what really kept me in it. I thought I hated my mind, that it was so ugly, that it was good for nothing except making people miserable, since most brainiacs I'd witnessed used their gifts to belittle, deride, and intimidate. I didn't want to be smart, because I equated it with being unkind, and not hot. Lucien knew this. He said, "We came together so we could both learn to live from the heart." This was why I had to be faithful, simple, true. "Cut the head," he'd say, whenever I displayed "too much mind," like if I pointed out flaws in his logic, his hypocrisies, or the other girls who announced themselves to me. "*Feel* what's *real*," he insisted.

At the core of feeling, at the core of me, as I imagine it is for everybody, is an infinite void full of love, ecstatic and soothing. I call it God, and while Lucien did help me learn to connect to this, claiming ownership over the discovery was perhaps his greatest cruelty. So colonial! As if. Lucien was constantly critiquing "the sins" of "the white man," but then he used language like the worst of them: seducing with flattering lies, claiming superiority through convoluted tautology and enigmatic vocabulary, then threatening violence when the previous tactics failed.

The great thing about being human, and not a character in a movie, is that, if you're doing it right, you're playing more than one role at a time. With Lucien, I may have been acting the part of a twentieth-century girl-form *attachée* to a Great Patriarch, a chick to his Manson, Anaïs to his Henry, Lee Krasnering his drippy Pollock, but I was also in concurrent relationships with my parents, my cat, my writing, my editors, and the girls.

I started picturing my girlfriends in the room when I was engaging with Lucien. Nadezhda was unimpressed by my laughing off his slut shaming. Susan rolled her disenchanted eyes so far back at his *yee-haw* they got stuck at her third eye and she became instantly enlightened. Clara saw herself in my letting Lucien coax desire out of me only to the point that it served his desire, and she stopped letting boys do that to her too. Mostly I kept thinking, *Amalia would've shot Lucien by now,* and that movie image—her cute Cupid lips pursed as she aimed a pistol at his entitled face—cracked me up and out of it. Amalia had better things to do than fuck with fuckboys. She was exhibiting at museums and galleries around the world, starring in movies in China, producing a cartoon for a network in the US, and editing two books.

It's messed up how being myself in public, like the idea of

ever publishing this book, still scares me more than a boy who breaks bottles in my face, punches his knuckles raw, and tells me I'm a sex addict just because I know how to communicate with the pulse of my my my!

Episode 12—"This is when the Real fun begins"

> There is no reality. There are only people who know this, and people who don't know this and are being manipulated by those who do.
>
> —TERENCE MCKENNA

NEITHER OF US COULD GET out of our own lives fast enough. I was about to turn thirty. Tracy was thirty-three, or thirty-four. She'd stopped counting. We wanted the same things.

"The world is trying to kill us," Tracy insisted, "with the erasure of magic."

"Yes," I said. "Reality is the most spiritual place, and few of us live here."

Our talk would flow fast and heavy, and we were miserable.

We were driving across the country, retracing the route my parents took with me in utero, thirty years ago to the week. It was Tracy who had to go. She had a wedding in Toronto and a solo show in New York after that. Then she was considering disappearing. Tracy has been miserable in Los Angeles. The real life she wanted there isn't possible. We're not rich, and she's lonely.

When I learned that Tracy was planning to drive to Canada alone, the creep of potential adventure took over. *I shouldn't go.* I had been in Baja. I had worked hard to get there. I had fumigated La Mariposa (roaches) so I could sublet my room (have cash). I had hired a cat-sitter for Noo, sold the last of my salable clothes, and gotten a pal to get a pal to get a pal to give me a ride to this self-made retreat (house-sitting again) where I was to write for and by myself, finally. I was almost thirty, and still talking to Lucien every now and again. He's sober and more responsible, but can still make me cum like I'm an angel as we're talking on the phone, and he knows about cool things, like plant subjectivity. He's also disappointing. All talk. He said he wanted to come to Baja just long enough for me to make him cum.

In Baja, I told Lucien, "I've been writing about us."

"Beautiful," he replied.

"You might not like it."

Pause.

"You could help"—I suggested—"make it a happy ending?" (It was always a battle of wills with us.) "I'd love to write a real modern romance."

The next day I Skyped my parents. *My parents.* I think about them every day, but rarely engage. With overbearing mothers of their own, they've let my brother and me more or less be since we were three. My parents wanted to talk because I mentioned the possible road trip in an e-mail and now they were all excited, almost romantic sounding.

"I can send you the exact route we took," my dad said. "You can stop in the park where your mother cried from exhaustion."

The road trip should've been fun, but I let everything that holds me back take up too much space in that car. Tracy likes to talk about trauma and hurt. We got into it early and I couldn't get back out. I was a slew of creepy relationships, I was getting off on conflict, I was maybe molested, defending my abuser, not standing up for myself, betraying my ideals, longing for Mom, never going be a mom; I was broke ... Was I poor? That's the word Tracy used: "I'm sorry that you're poor."

One night we had to spend one hundred dollars more than I expected on a hotel. We'd just left Boulder, Colorado, where all the cute hippie B and Bs were booked. We drove from motel to hotel to motel—all sold out. The parking lots were stuffed with shiny new pickup trucks and SUVs. "Oilmen," the night clerk at one Ramada Inn explained. "There's oil work right now." At eleven p.m., after twelve hours of driving, we finally found a suite to sleep in. It was my turn to pay, and because it was more than I'd budgeted for, I spun out as I do when I'm around people: *wordlessly.*

I know what set me off. It was early in our journey, and

Tracy had suggested, as she had a few times before, that I "be more empathetic," that this would somehow solve all my problems. I got defensive and then I was silent. Neil Young played. Unspoken rebuttals rushed in: *I know I was closed off for a decade plus. I know I can seem cold and disconnected, but I believe it's because I am an empath.*

I feel what you feel, and it can engulf me. That's why sex is so epic and why living in New York was so hard—too many competing energies, I couldn't filter the feels. Empathy is a liability in this country: it's inefficient, unproductive, and I'm paranoid. Sober around drunks, I'll feel that loosening, mean heat. Sober around stoners, I'll get goofy, cushy, cloudy. Migraines are contagious, as are hysteria, mania, and lethargy. When Noo gnaws on her claws, I feel this satisfying pushback of kitty cuticles, like we're one entity.

As we approached the Canadian border and crossed into Sarnia, Ontario—exactly as my parents did with me thirty years ago—Tracy and I felt lifted. The sky was the same, but as Tracy said, "Isn't it like a dark cloud has passed?" It was true: life felt lighter here.

"I could speed and get pulled over and not be afraid!" Tracy wowed.

"We could get in an accident," I added. "And go to the hospital!"

Windows down: we loved the smell of rural Ontario, and talked about moving back to Canada. But just a couple of hours later, as we were entering Toronto, it became "Ummm, no, I don't think so. Ha ha ha." (This is a common question for ambitious Canadians: Why do so few of us stay?)

I had kept going back to that house. The one my parents and Lucien all lived in. I'd hitch my bike to public buses and ride two and half hours from La Mariposa to Malibu and cry in front of the locked gate, the house now owned by some rich tech exec, like an encroaching amount of Westside real estate.

Once, when I was twelve, my parents took my brother and me to Southern California for a family funeral, and we passed by their old home.

"We made you right below that window—" my dad said, pointing to a jutting construction.

"Oh yeah," my mom deadpanned. "I know exactly when it happened."

No wonder I grew up to be a pervert.

They got married in that house too. My mom wore Japanese designers, powder pink and sapphire blue. They had ten friends over, a woman priest presiding, and served sushi and champagne.

"Does it bother you that it wasn't Real?" Tracy asked me on our trip. Her last relationship had also been this kind of thing: an entitled white male artist who gets girls to play roles he basically scripts for them. Absurd sex. Demeaning critiques. A totalizing experience. They tell you you're special, say "I love you," when really, you're one of what have been, and will be, many.

"No," I replied. "Because it was real to me."

God knows I love a good story. Synchronicity compels me. That's why God gave me this coincidence: so I'd get in that car with Tracy. A Saturn Return retrace, LA to Toronto, was too juicy not to follow. Even though it was painful (there were times when I wanted to smother Tracy, for all our drive was reminding me of), I stayed the course, and eventually was delivered to where I needed to be.

From my parents' apartment in Toronto, I could see how I'd spent the last two years crying in front of the wrong door. I'd been trying to make a home out of a broken American boy, when I should've been addressing where I'm blessed to have come from. Where I probably chose to be born.

I get it! If I got knocked up now, I'd move back to Canada too.

"It's just like the US," my Midwestern friend Katherine said on her first visit to my homeland. "Only no one's evil here."

When I got back to Los Angeles, thirty years old now (it happened in Toronto), it was time to move out of La Mariposa.

There'd been a series of subletters all summer, as Nadezhda, Darya, and I came and went. The young woman who had been occupying my room had somehow turned my white sheets sooty, ashen, and green. There were tiny pieces of torn paper and dust bunnies all over; roaches tickling the bathroom floor.

This subletter had extended her destruction as far as the apartment's front door when she was locked out one evening. Nadezhda had texted her, *Wait! I'll be home in an hour.* But this impatient punk decided to kick down the door instead. Nadezhda, with her surveillance paranoia, was always complaining about the security cameras in our halls, but I love picturing it: a grainy long-shot of this young woman's strong tattooed leg cracking down our once-dear front door.

My new place is on the Westside, the sunny home of a young man named Brandon, who, like my father's friend from when they were our age, suffered irreparable physical injury while working construction for the art world. Brandon was burned while assisting a young male artist who hasn't touched a piece of art, except to sign it, since he was signed to a blue-chip gallery at twenty-three.

Like most of my friends, Brandon didn't have health insurance, and the young artist he worked for didn't have workplace insurance; he was paying everyone under the table. Brandon was being paid fifteen bucks an hour to work with hot wax and light steel. He was assembling some sort of militaristic ventriloquist-dummy-cum-drone in the guise of Icarus. The artist Brandon worked for wanted to fly his dummy over the beach at Miami Art Basel. He called "the whole tableau" "a painting." It was about "climate change, surveillance, and the will to power," or something. When Brandon incurred third-degree burns on his hands, feet, and face, along with tens of thousands in hospital bills, from a faulty hot wax container, he sued his employer for personal injury. The artist countersued for defamation; he said he'd never hired Brandon. The cases kept getting stalled, Brandon couldn't afford his lawyer, and now he has legal debt on top of the medical, and is looking for someone to come on board pro bono.

My father's friend Michael fell down an empty, unmarked elevator shaft in a minor art star's New York City loft when he was doing repairs for the artist in the mid-'80s. My father moved to Point Dume, Malibu, to assist Michael through physical and cognitive rehab. That's how he met my mother.

Not only does Brandon, an LA native, know dozens of women who have fallen for Lucien Langham (and at least three of them at the same time as me), but he also makes everything seem so simple. "Life is difficult enough as it is," he says. "There's no use adding stress to stress." For every girl Lucien has chewed through, Brandon has a friend. His friends are always coming over to lend him a hand since his are out of commission.

I think the most dangerous thing about not feeling Real, which I still often don't, is that you're liable to treat others that way. When I "quit writing," it was for the same reason I killed the reality show contract: I was afraid of doing harm.

I was six years old in a party dress when I learned how evil I can be. It was one of those exhilarating first days of spring in Montreal, and we were playing in the park after school. I was playing alone, climbing a favorite tree, which I realized, as I got

settled in on a high branch, was covered in fuzzy green cater-
pillars. Hundreds of black-spotted green creatures with orange
antennae. They crawled all over me. Their prolegs were sticky,
like tiny damp suction cups. I kissed a few on my fingers and
placed them back on the branches, as delicately as I could. For
what felt like a long time, I was in awe of their quantity. I whis-
pered stories to them, named them, and tickled them against
my cheeks, like butterfly kisses from my baby brother. When
my mom called me to go, I shimmied down the tree as usual.
On the ground, I saw how my dress was maimed. Splotches of
green and yellow were crushed into its full pale skirt. The horror
crawled up my back too. I must've killed dozens of new friends
in my play.

The reality show was too much like the writing I do. Jour-
nalistic, invasive. Writers are evil. Our material is this world,
is people, is power, is love. If I'm not murdering, I'm at least a
thief. I can't make art without stealing. People are my favorite
medium.

Cats are evil, too, and I love them. So maybe it's okay that I
am what I am. We're predators, daydreamers, slinky, dethroned
royalty, cuddly only when we say.

But Tracy was right about the empathy thing: I'm not the
compassionate creature I wish I were. For years, I've pictured
myself hugging, double-kissing, teasing, cuddling, and giving
love. Instead I wear what Simone dubbed my "turtle shell." It's
more like Bowser's shell, from Super Mario Bros. My armor is
spiky-sharp, untouchable, and it weighs on me.

During our road trip, I kept looking at Tracy's back, hunched

over the wheel. She had done all the driving, four thousand ki-
lometers in four days, because her car insurance was expired,
I'd only just gotten my license, and she didn't want to risk more
than she already was. I wanted to help. She was obviously in
pain, wincing, rolling her shoulders and neck. I kept thinking:
Rub her back. I kept picturing it and I couldn't do it. My turtle
shell had turned into a straitjacket. *Do it. Don't do it. Why can't
I do it?*

I'll always be in that silver sedan with Tracy, unable to reach
out, just as I'll always be on the ground by that tree, gutted by
the evil inside me.

In the weeks before our road trip, I visited Tracy in her studio
often. She was putting the final touches on the pieces for her
solo show. Ambitious, huge canvases. Those roses covered by
black blinds, and butterflies. Tracy cut hundreds of butterflies
out of canvas and painted them sunflower yellow, pumpkin,
chalkboard black, shimmery mauve, and many tones of rose.
She affixed at least one butterfly to every piece in her show. One
canvas was covered in them. A flurry of asymmetrical maripo-
sas, as if every freak we knew were flying free.

We were turned on—lit up—by screens. They'd raised us.
Which was why I thought our real *Real World* might work. It
was a bad idea though. Don't worry—I'm full of them. If I could

only sell my soul, I'd make a great ad executive. I know exactly what to sell: *desire.*

Nadezhda tells me she wishes she'd "never asked 'Why?' So you wouldn't have doubted, so it could've happened . . ." Two Leo Moons, we talk about the spell of "And . . . action!" How cameras alert to the moment. This is the appeal: we want to feel pushed up against the Real. *Here and now, wow!* I've been practicing delivering this with my everyday gaze: shining it upon the world, upon my people, who and what I want to see play. It's like David—the boy from the desert; remember? he's now a film producer—said to me: "You're the camera, Fiona."

Even when days on end are gray and nights are rife with nightmares, I'm grateful that electrical outlets look like little spooked faces; amused that you can almost spell *evil* with *beautiful*; and mesmerized by how a person can change you. I hated gray days until I loved Tracy. Now I get a thrill in them, imagining how she'd feel—alert under gray as I am under the sun.

I wanted to give the young residents of La Mariposa everything I thought I'd missed. I wished someone had taken my amorphous anxiety seriously. I wished I'd been gently called out for being a phony. I wished someone had loved me enough to ask, "What do you want?" And, "Do you know how to want?" And if not—the answer would've been no—I wished someone would've taught me.

The Real is like getting to exist in my truth. Which is like, ultimately, we don't know what the fuck we're doing here so let's make the best of it. All my youthful suffering—my shame, meekness, mania, depression, dysphoria, hysteria—I now think of as an existential, or spiritual, misunderstanding.

See, for a long time, I thought I was missing something. Everyone else around me seemed to function like they knew what was going on, like they had purpose, direction, a role. I'd go through phases where I'd try to imitate people who seemed near enough to my makeup and who were making it in the world. It never worked. That's when I'd come across as a phony. Or I'd rescind it all, go blank—hide out in my home or mask my void under spectacular clothes. *They must know something I don't know,* I thought. I was constantly doubting myself. I'd misplaced my conscious intuitive faculties, like so many of us do.

It took me a long time to embrace a thing like God. What I now know of it is so private, I hardly want to speak on it. As a young girl, I feared even trying to believe. I was afraid—the same way I was with schoolyard bullies, cops, doctors, girl crushes, and my parents—of looking foolish and being punished, or worse, dismissed. "God" to me then was but a historical concept, a means to justify oppression and repression, man over other, righteousness; at best, it seemed like a consolation prize for the dispossessed. The word irked me. *God dog God dog God dog.*

A lot of words I didn't get until I got them. When I was flailing in my early twenties, Simone would tell me, "Trust your gut." She'd ask, "What does your heart say?" I'd shake my head. I didn't know how to understand what she was suggesting.

I was raised cold, with little exposure to felt experiences of *heart, gut,* or *soul.* David sent me a passage the other day about the word *cliché.* It comes from, this article suggested, the sound typewriters make. A word or phrase, typed too many times, became a *Clich-ay Clich-ay Clich-ay.* Saying the words out loud now—*gut, God, heart, soul, spirit, truth*—I feel their reality rise, in the same way that if I hear *Fifi* in a crowded space, I sit at attention and look for its source. Try it with different words:

Love. *Love love love.* I love saying *love!* It's enveloping. Easy. Like a smile across my heart center. And *potency?* Doesn't it sound just like *engorgement?* Like pride. Like ooooh, baby, oh. Potent! Potential!

When I'm in a fury, I swear. I curse. People get hurt. *Cursing.* See? Once we understood the magic of words.

Even though La Mariposa said they trusted me, I knew there was something creepy about my desire to put them on display. It was classic confused Leo meets Virgo. A little dictator— exhibitionist, slavish, savior complex. Instead of addressing what needed to be addressed—ha ha, *me*—I sought to work through others, to transform the world.

My hair is about six inches longer. That's the most marked material change between when I first moved to LA at twenty-eight and now at thirty. That and I can drive a car. Not that I can afford one. I'm still walking this city like I'm fucking Socrates. I have thick calves and knees. I've walked hundreds of hours in Fendi wood-soled clogs, Prada Sport kitten heels, Eckhaus Latta platforms, and my Lucchese cowboy boots. I walk, think, listen, and look.

Nadezhda got rid of her motorcycle. She worked hard to get

her grades up at community college, so she could qualify for this BFA program she wanted to go to at UCLA. She got in. She got a car. She got a boyfriend, they broke up. She started studying hacking for real in her free time, and is traveling in Russia right now. Alicia's been waitressing and writing in New York. She quit modeling. She blocked that abusive ex-boyfriend. She's mid–Saturn Returning, and confused—it's a confusing time! Morgan flexed her way back to sociability, a state like peace, and moved to Amsterdam to finish her undergraduate degree. Maxime I keep seeing at the back of these readings I started hosting. I've seen him at events in LA and New York and I swear I saw his bleached mane in Montreal. As for Miffany, I don't know. She dropped offline completely, so I only hear rumors about her sometimes.

Simone, now thirty-two, has been painting church ceilings. She founded her own art restoration business, and has a calendar of work ahead of her. I visited her on-site in Saint Francis Church in Toronto a couple months ago. She had me—scared of heights—climb the scaffolding all the way to the top, where we shared a half bottle of Barolo, ate soft cheeses, and gossiped. Mo's been having an affair with her hot young Sicilian assistant! He's the one who suggested I call her Simone in my book.

Amalia keeps voyaging to China. Her Mandarin's even better than her Russian now, and her Russian's not bad. Tracy, I miss. Clara too. They're both living blocks from their family homes, in Victoria, Canada, and La Crosse, Wisconsin.

Darya and I had a falling-out. She's an actress, remember? She was the one who informed me that "a *casa de mariposa* means 'a whorehouse.'" One of the last conversations we had was about Lucien. Her favorite parts of this book were about him. I was wondering, after reading Sarah Schulman's *Conflict Is Not Abuse*, if I'd overstated Lucien's harm. Schulman writes about how abusers often claim they're being abused as a way to stake more power. "Maybe," I mused to Darya, "I was confused. Maybe by thinking I was a victim, I abused my power?" Darya swiftly replied: "When have you ever been in a position of power, Fiona?"

I learn so many new things every day, I'm always thinking about how stupid I must still be!

On my thirtieth birthday, I had thrown a temper tantrum. I was so ashamed about not being the adult I wanted to be yet. I had to borrow money from a friend for rent that week. "Why am I such a loser?" I embodied my upset, and acted like a kid.

Two months of introspection later, I threw myself a belated birthday party, because how else are you going to get what you want? I made two cakes, hosted two dozen friends, and served cheap prosecco, grilled asparagus, and monkfish. Amalia gifted me soap made by priests, and Alana, a thirty-three-year-old children's librarian, gave me a birthday card that read: *Welcome to your 30s, Fiona! This is when the real fun begins . . .*

A couple of months later, I met Miranda. Miranda, the girl who unmade my bed with Clara while I was dying in Mexico. Her fairylike laugh rang out at an event I was attending. She was the one who asked to hang out. Dubious but curious, I invited her to a party at a strip club later that night, but by the time she got there, I was gone.

We rain-checked for a sunny day in early February. She showed up at my place in black silk gauchos embroidered with butterflies. She wore opals on three of her fingers, matching my own most precious family heirloom. Our hair was center-parted and hippie stringy at the ends. Her skin is rosewood to my porcelain.

I like Miranda. She has the same oozy need-to-be-loved energy as Lucien, but she tries for it by giving it. This radiant magnetism that I know how to give off too, but I rarely do because I know it can attract the wrong kind of attention. She is also incredibly smart, with an enviable memory for factual detail. Her character flaw, she said, believably, when I asked her, "would have to be being too trusting."

Within a few hangs, I learned that Miranda had been sexually abused, more often even than Clara, and that she was only just starting to conceive of these experiences as nonconsensual, after a friend witnessed one in a threesome, and suggested it was messed up. It was normal until then, dating to back before puberty. Daddy and big-brother types taking advantage.

When I revealed to Miranda that I was involved with Lucien when she was too, she acted surprised, like: "No way! Wow. Just wow."

I asked her what it was like, and she confirmed that she, too, was told she was loved; told she was needed; told if she left him, she'd be responsible for killing him. She, too, Miranda told me, felt for Lucien, big feels, nurturing mother stuff, and so she would engage, then not, because when she did, her life would twist into chaos, confusion, paranoia, and isolation. Miranda also, like me, admitted she'd been consistently attracted to boys and men who, like Lucien, showed off obvious power, access, and prestige. "They're all assholes," she conceded.

Right after Miranda and I traded our first set of Lucien stories, she tried on a strap-on I had just been gifted. We were in my bedroom. It was a velvet thong harness with an eight-inch dildo. Blush-pink tip. She put the thing on over her butterfly pants and waved her hips around, so the dual-density shaft slapped at her thighs, and we laughed.

"I've always felt like I was a boy," Miranda told me then, and I replied, "Me too," not revealing that once or more, the year before, I got off imagining myself as Lucien fucking her, the other girl.

I love Los Angeles because it's a never-ending story. There's always something new in bloom. No winter death mourning. The apocalypse has already happened. It feels like heaven and hell. You get to exist on this eternal current, attentive to the subtlest seasonal changes, like jacaranda and jasmine in spring, and June gloom, the only time when our *Truman Show*–bubble blue sky is constantly overwhelmed.

The first year I lived in Los Angeles, I'd race out of the house to see the raw pink sunset every night. "Culture's still nature!" I'd rebut, whenever someone tried to discount the vivid beauty I was in awe of because "it's only like that because of pollution."

My parents moved me between three cities and nine homes

before I was eight years old, more if you count in utero. I lived in fifteen apartments in five years before landing in Los Angeles, and I traveled. I felt unsettled whenever I wasn't in motion. In LA, I found a city where I could be closer to still, or maybe it's more like: it's so sprawling, you're kind of always traveling. I get meditative, calm, en route.

I don't get too attached to places, I think, because they stay with me. For whatever reason, streets and buildings stick in my memory when little else does. I can close my eyes and move through every home I've occupied. I know to avoid the slippery step in the basement of the big house in Ottawa from my teen years, just as I could draw the gemlike construction of the walls in the bathroom of this apartment in Montreal that my mom and I leased for two years.

La Mariposa had an expansive ceiling. It was so high, you almost felt like you were outdoors, or in another world. At the same time, the apartment was cocoon-like, safe. The bathrooms were pink. There were ten large windows—two in each wing, and six in the center room—all along the same wall. Nadezhda used to live in what became my bedroom. She put holographic tape on the windows that cast rainbows when the sun hit just right: three p.m. in winter, four to six throughout the rest of the year.

I've been writing the last few episodes of this book through a cracked screen on my laptop, which regularly crashes, forcing a restart. The crack was an accident. A crystal dildo, slippery from use, slipped out of my hand while I was dancing in my bedroom, and smashed into my screen. The crack has been expanding. Now it's more like a portal. A palm-size black pool with purple and green glitches around it that keeps growing, spreading, infecting my workplace.

Knowing I'm still struggling to make rent, no car, stranded West, with half a computer, and since I mentioned "I suck at endings, everything always keeps going," Nadezhda started offering to end the lease at La Mariposa, "so you'll have a conclusion for your book."

I told her, "No. Do it in your own time," neglecting to say what I meant: "I'm touched by your offering."

The day I declared this book done (I wrote a fine-enough final line), Darya announced she was moving to New York and Nadezhda into student housing. They'd already given notice on La Mariposa, forging my signature on their letter to release, because even though I'd moved out five months ago, I was still technically on the lease.

Acknowledgments

Thank you, Alana, Alex, Alexa, Alexis, Alicia, Allie, Amalia, Amanda Yates Garcia (the Oracle of LA, for her information on egregores), Amber, Ana, Ana Grace, Anastasia, Anna Jane, Asher, Beastlet, Bobby, Brant, Chloe, Chris, Dean, Durga, Eric, Fabiola, Flan, Henry, Ian, Ingo, Jac, Jacky, Janique, John, Jordan, Leslie, Malcolm, Margaret, Marsha, Martha, Matt, Matthew, Michelle, Monique, Noo, Riane, Rose, Sarah, Sojourner, Sra, Stefan, Steven, Vejas, Vivian, and Yuka: this couldn't have happened without you.

"If you described it to me, there's no way I would read it. It's everything I hate in life and literature, but somehow it's really good." —DEAN KISSICK, *Spike Magazine*

"*Exquisite Mariposa* is one of those books that had me from the first sentence to the last and beyond. Duncan churns up all the digital, performative, hypersocial chaos of our present 'reality,' even of the near future, and crystallizes it into dreamy and raw poetry. Page after page, paragraph after paragraph, this story, built on jewellike insights, sometimes made me laugh and sometimes made me sad and always registered as true." —JARDINE LIBAIRE, author of *White Fur*

"An unapologetically raw account of coming of age broke in Trump-era Los Angeles in the social media–saturated Now, this meditation (almost manifesto?) on materialism, media, power, performance, and sexuality uses inventive, of-the-moment language to tackle that circuitous route to self-discovery that is your twenties—in a startlingly original way." —LILIBET SNELLINGS, author of *Box Girl: My Part Time Job as an Art Installation*

"A funny, thought-provoking novel that levels pointed critiques at gender and class inequality and captures what it's like to be a young person today . . . The novel's ideas and voice are a pleasure . . . *Exquisite Mariposa* is an incisive story about the struggles of sensitive, artistic young people as they figure out how best to live." —REBECCA HUSSEY, *Foreword Reviews*

Praise for *Exquisite Mariposa*

"Ecstatic and painful, *Exquisite Mariposa* is a diligent search for the heart of The Real, taking its place alongside the great Young Girl books of becoming, from Mary McCarthy's *The Company She Keeps* to Sally Rooney's *Conversations with Friends*. To Duncan, The Real equals self-knowledge, compassion, and perception. She is a genius, and I'd follow her anywhere."

—CHRIS KRAUS, author of *After Kathy Acker* and *I Love Dick*

"*Exquisite Mariposa* is like if Eve Babitz wrote *Weetzie Bat*: luminous, loopy, magical, and picaresque. It's an honor to even live in the same Los Angeles that this book describes."

—CLAIRE L. EVANS, author of *Broad Band: The Untold Story of the Women Who Made the Internet*

"Fiona Alison Duncan will raise your consciousness and spirits with her unworldly presence, her sensuous and intense perception, her free-floating mind. She may be an alien, but she is a friendly, peace-seeking alien who just wants to talk. I could listen to her voice all day." —SARAH NICOLE PRICKETT, founding editor of *Adult*, contributor to *Artforum* and *Bookforum*